Wedding Bells at Lake Como

The perfect destination for love!

Italy's picturesque Lake Como is the perfect destination for love, except the path to happy-ever-after isn't always smooth...

Cousins Gianna and Carla aren't looking for romance. Gianna's nursing a broken heart and Carla's wed to the family business. Until charismatic brothers Dario and Franco arrive on Lake Como's stunning shores...and sweep them off their feet!

Find out what happens when a case of mistaken identity leads to a fake engagement in *Bound by a Ring and a Secret*

And discover Carla and Franco's story in *Falling for Her Convenient Groom*

Available now!

Dear Reader,

Sometimes when you love someone so much, you'll do whatever it takes to keep them safe— even taking drastic measures. That's exactly what happens to restaurateur Carla Falco when her workaholic father refuses to listen to his doctors and slow down. There's one thing her father wants above all else—Carla to get married. She uses this to her advantage and strikes a most unusual deal with her father. And then she proposes to the grandson of her father's archenemy, knowing he dislikes marriage even more than she does. Theirs will be a union of purely business.

Spice merchant Franco Marchello has less than zero interest in marriage, but he's getting desperate to save his family's faltering business. So when beautiful and alluring Carla surprises him with a most unique marriage proposal, he's absolutely torn about what to do.

But as they work together and get to know each other better, will they be able to ignore their growing feelings and stay focused on the business at hand? Because a marriage on paper only might sound like a good idea in theory but everything changes after saying "I do."

Happy reading,

Jennifer

Falling for Her Convenient Groom

Jennifer Faye

HARLEQUIN

Romance

Recycling programs
for this product may
not exist in your area.

ISBN-13: 978-1-335-40676-7

Falling for Her Convenient Groom

Copyright © 2021 by Jennifer F. Stroka

This edition published by arrangement with Harlequin Books S.A.

For questions and comments about the quality of this book,
please contact us at CustomerService@Harlequin.com.

Harlequin Enterprises ULC
22 Adelaide St. West, 40th Floor
Toronto, Ontario M5H 4E3, Canada
www.Harlequin.com

Printed in U.S.A.

Award-winning author **Jennifer Faye** pens
fun, heartwarming contemporary romances
with rugged cowboys, sexy billionaires and
enchanting royalty. Internationally published
with books translated into nine languages, she
is a two-time winner of the *RT Book Reviews*
Reviewers' Choice Award. She has also won the
CataRomance Reviewers' Choice Award, been
named a Top Pick author and been nominated
for numerous other awards.

Books by Jennifer Faye

Harlequin Romance

Wedding Bells at Lake Como

Bound by a Ring and a Secret

The Bartolini Legacy

The Prince and the Wedding Planner
The CEO, the Puppy and Me
The Italian's Unexpected Heir

Once Upon a Fairytale

Beauty and Her Boss
Miss White and the Seventh Heir
Fairytale Christmas with the Millionaire

Snowbound with an Heiress
Her Christmas Pregnancy Surprise

Visit the Author Profile page
at Harlequin.com for more titles.

PROLOGUE

Verona, Italy

SHE WAS IN CHARGE.

It hadn't been her goal. She had been satisfied with working in the background.

Still, Carla Falco now sat in the CEO's chair, and it was time to sign off on the payroll for the Falco Fresco Ristorante empire. Her gaze moved down over the sizable disbursement requisition, making sure everything looked in order—

The office door burst open. She glanced up to see her father stride into the room with a frown on his face. For a man who'd had two heart attacks in less than a year with the most recent one barely two weeks ago, he certainly didn't look feeble. In fact, he reminded her of a charging bull with steam emanating from his nostrils.

He wasn't supposed to be here. He was supposed to be at home, following the doctor's orders of modest exercise and a lean, wholesome diet. More importantly, he was supposed to be relaxing instead of stressing over the family business. That was her job now.

"How could you do it?" His voice boomed through the large office.

She stood and moved to the door. She caught her assistant, Rosa's, surprised look and sent her a reassuring smile before closing the door so they could have this conversation in private instead of having the whole office hear them. Then she turned to him. "I suppose you're referring to halting the expansion into Sicily."

"Yes! We talked about this. I told you I wanted to build there."

"And after looking at the numbers, as well as consulting with department heads, I have to disagree with you. We need to focus on our current properties. Many are now older and in need of updating."

His face filled with color. He was so worked up he couldn't speak. She'd known he wouldn't be happy about the decision, but she was hoping he wouldn't hear about it for a while. In fact, she'd gone to great lengths to keep this information under wraps, but it appeared her father had a mole in the company. Why didn't that surprise her?

She moved to his side and then gestured to one of the two black leather armchairs facing her desk. "Sit down."

He didn't say anything for a moment. Then

he moved to the other side of the desk and sat down in her chair. "I think sitting down is exactly what I should do."

"Papa, what are you doing?"

"I'm taking over my position as CEO once more. Your services are no longer needed."

Her mouth gaped as her mind struggled to make sense of what had just happened. "You're firing me?"

His gaze narrowed in on her. "I'm giving you time to concentrate on your life."

"This is my life."

"No. This is my life. You need to go find your own." His voice was firm.

"But you're in no condition to return to work. You should be at home resting."

"I've rested. All I do is rest. I'm done resting."

His definition of rest and hers were two different things. He showed up at the office every day, looking over her shoulder and questioning everything. If she didn't do something quickly to change things, she would never win the respect of the employees now reporting to her. She would be ineffectual as the CEO, and her father's beloved company would flounder.

Not to mention that every time her father visited the office, he got worked up over something. These were the details he didn't need to concern himself with at the moment. His focus should be on his precarious health and how to strengthen his body.

Her mind raced for a way to fix the situation. She knew what her father wanted more than anything—for her to marry. It was an idea she'd been toying with lately. Maybe she could make a deal of sorts.

"What would you say if I was willing to make you a deal?" She knew her father thrived on wheeling and dealing—the higher the stakes, the more he enjoyed it.

He paused for a moment as though he was trying to figure out her angle. Then, in a more normal tone of voice, he asked, "What sort of deal?"

"What if I agree to get married?"

His eyes lit up with interest. "I'd say it was about time. Who is it? Fernando from dinner last night?" He rubbed his chin. "Or perhaps it is Edwardo that caught your eye."

"You're rushing ahead." She had him on the hook. Now she just had to keep him there.

His gaze narrowed. "I know that look in your eyes. You're up to something."

"I'm just being a businesswoman."

He grunted. "Leave the business up to me. You have other matters to worry about."

"Ah, yes, marriage. What are you willing to sacrifice in order to see me married?"

"Sacrifice?" His shocked tone reverberated

off the tall walls with their floor-to-ceiling windows and various watercolor paintings of Italian life. "What is it you want in exchange?"

"I want you to hand over the reins of the company for—" she rushed to think of an appropriate length of time "—a year."

He didn't move. He didn't even blink. He just stared at her. Though she knew him well enough to know the wheels in his mind were turning. He was trying to figure out how to work this in his favor—how he could get everything he wanted. But it wouldn't work. Not this time.

He shook his head. "Not a year. A month."

She pressed her hands to her hips. She could be just as stubborn as him. "A month isn't enough time to rearrange the furniture in this office."

His silver brows rose high on his forehead. "You're going to change the office? But I love it the way it is—"

"No, I'm not." She sighed. "That was just a figure of speech. But you know exactly what I mean. I need more than a month. You need more time to recuperate."

He shook his head. "When you get married, you're supposed to concentrate on your husband. Not spend all your time in the office."

"You let me worry about my marriage and my office hours. But since you aren't interested in negotiating, let's forget it. I have work to do in my office. It's time you went home." She turned for the door, all the while hoping he would stop her. "After all, the doctor hasn't released you for work."

She took slow, measured steps to the door. She thought of stopping and speaking to him, but she knew her father was a shrewd poker player. He would see a bluff from a long way off if she wasn't careful. And it wasn't truly a bluff. If he went for this deal, she would be getting married. The thought sent dread skittering down her spine. But she would deal with that if or when the time came.

"Okay." The resigned tone of his voice said that she had won. "Three months."

She didn't immediately turn; she hesitated just for a second or two, just like any good negotiator would do. Because he might be her father, but he was a businessman first, last and always.

She needed time to implement her plan to modernize the restaurant chain. She'd already been in talks with various department heads. But it was going to take a long time to give hundreds of restaurants makeovers.

When she faced him, she said, "Six months." It would give her enough time to firm up a plan and start the renovations on a couple of restaurants—enough to show her father what a difference it would make to their patrons and eventually their bottom line. When he went to negotiate further, she cut him off. "Six months, not a day less, or the deal is null and void. And I want this in writing."

And then her father smiled. "You do have your father in you. Nicely played. Now who is the man you've chosen to marry?"

"All in due time. First, we have a contract to draw up. The rest will follow."

It was only then that she let the reality of this deal sink in. She was getting married. She was about to marry someone she didn't love. She was in so much trouble.

CHAPTER ONE

Two weeks later

"MARRY ME."

Seated in a little out-of-the-way café on the outskirts of Verona, Franco Marchello wordlessly opened his mouth. He immediately forgot what he'd been about to say. Surely he hadn't heard correctly. Because there was absolutely no way Carla Falco had proposed to him.

Still, he'd seen her glossy red lips move. The words she'd spoken, he must have gotten them mixed up. That was it. His mind raced to come up with an alternative: Carry me? Bury me? None of the alternatives made a bit of sense.

Franco swallowed hard. "Excuse me, what did you say?"

Carla didn't smile. In fact, she looked quite serious, the way he imagined seeing her at the head of the table in a boardroom. "I asked you to marry me."

That's what he thought she'd said. And yet he had no idea why she'd propose to him.

Sure, they might have had a good time at his brother's wedding two weeks ago at Lake Como. She had been the maid of honor and he'd been the best man, but that had been one evening of laughter and dancing. Maybe he hadn't wanted the evening to end so soon, but Carla had avoided his attempts to turn the evening into something more intimate. So what had changed her mind?

The following week, he'd invited her to dinner. She'd been hesitant until he assured her that it would be a proper business dinner. After all, she'd rebuffed him once. He wasn't about to subject himself to being rejected twice—no matter how beautiful he found her or how her glossy lips tempted him. He made it abundantly clear that the only thing on his mind was a mutually beneficial business arrangement.

Even though it'd been dinner for two, as promised, he'd kept it all aboveboard. He'd pitched her the reason she should consider putting Marchello Spices back in all her family's restaurants. She'd told him she didn't have the authority to make it happen. Her father was still controlling every aspect of the company. But she had been curious enough to agree to review the projections. He knew if she saw the same potential that he'd seen in those numbers, she wouldn't be able to ignore them. At last, he had an in with her father, who'd refused numerous times to meet with him—all because of an old grudge between him and Franco's grandfather.

And that's where things had ended—on the sidewalk outside the café. Had there been something in his drink that evening? Had he blacked out and totally forgotten about some torrid romantic night together—anything to explain this most unexpected proposal?

Because he didn't do marriage—no way. He was a Marchello. Marchellos were notoriously bad at marriage. At least his parents had been.

But then again, his younger brother had just gotten married. That was what had initially led Franco directly into Carla's orbit. And they'd been running into each other ever since. Now it seemed as though the entire world had completely and utterly rotated off its axis.

He struggled to swallow. His brain raced to find the right words. "Why do you want to get married?"

He purposely failed to include himself in that question. Maybe she just wanted to get married to anyone and he just happened to be standing in the wrong place at the wrong time.

She glanced away. "Perhaps I jumped a bit ahead."

"You think?" When his words caused her to frown, he quieted down. Now that the shock had worn off a bit, he was anxious to hear what this was all about.

She toyed with the spoon resting on the saucer next to her teacup. "My father isn't well."

"I heard about his heart attack the night of my brother's wedding. How's he doing?"

"The doctors have warned him that if he doesn't slow down and watch his diet, the prognosis isn't good."

"I'm sorry to hear that." Now he understood the impromptu proposal. "And you want to get married to make him happy, in case something happens?"

"No. I want to get married so nothing happens to him."

He had absolutely no idea what any of this had to do with him. As far as he knew, her father hated not just him but his whole family. "But surely you have a boyfriend to marry."

"If I did, do you really think I'd propose to you?"

Okay, so he was still missing something. "Our families hate each other." He shook his head. "This is a very bad idea."

The story went that his grandfather and Carla's father used to be good friends. They would play cards at their private club. But Carla's father started drinking a lot and his gambling got out of control—so much so that he risked his restaurant empire. Desperate not to lose everything, Carlo Falco cheated at cards. And the two men haven't spoken since.

Carla crossed her arms. "If your grandfather hadn't lied about my father—"

"He didn't." Franco stopped himself just in time, because if he'd said more, he knew it would hurt Carla, and she didn't deserve it.

She blindly loved her father, oblivious to his faults. Who was he to steal that from her? Franco knew what it was to live without a father's love. He didn't want to be the one to drive a wedge between Carla and her father.

She arched a brow at him. "Stands to reason you'd be on your grandfather's side."

Anything he said about the ill feelings between their families was just going to make matters worse. And it wasn't helping him understand Carla's sudden proposal.

"I'm confused. Why you think we should get married?" He gazed at her until she glanced away.

"My father refuses to let me run the company as I see fit, even though I have a business degree that is doing nothing more than collecting dust. He's more intent on having me plan his social functions while he works on finding me the appropriate husband—someone who can step in and run his company."

"And you think I can run his company on top of managing my own family business?"

A frown pulled at her beautiful face as her gaze met his once more. "Certainly not."

"Then I still don't understand."

She sighed and glanced out the window at the bustling piazza. "My father is resistant to hand over the reins of the company to me, even though he's had a massive heart attack." She failed to mention the most recent heart attack as she'd promised her father to keep it quiet. "Instead he spends all his time parading men in front of me, hoping I'll choose one to marry."

"So I was right." He'd warned her about her father's matchmaking at his brother's wedding to her cousin.

"Yes. I confronted him, and the rumors are true." She didn't sound happy about it. "He started this matchmaking before he'd had his heart attack, but now he's gone into overdrive. So in order for me to be able to pick my own husband and also to prove to my father that I'm quite capable of running the business, I've negotiated a deal with him. According to our agreement, I have until the end of the year to marry. If I don't marry by then, the deal is null and void. But I don't intend to waste any time with the formalities. Once I'm married, I can run the company any way I see fit for the following six months."

"You arranged a marriage contract?" He

didn't know if he should be awed by her or worried about her.

"In a manner of speaking. All with the best of intentions." Then her big brown eyes turned to him. "So, will you do it? Will you marry me?"

Her insides were knotted up with nervous energy.

Carla couldn't believe she'd been pushed into this unbelievably awkward position. She'd never imagined she'd be marrying for business, not love. But if she didn't do something drastic, she feared her father would work himself to death, quite literally. Just the thought made her heart clench.

And though she was marrying someone that her father would be totally opposed to, she knew if her father gave Franco a chance, he would see what she'd seen—that Franco was a good guy. If he wasn't someone she could reasonably trust and respect, she wouldn't have made this totally outrageous proposition.

Buzz. Buzz.

Her gaze moved to her phone that was quietly resting on the table. Even though it was the same ringtone, it was Franco's phone going off. She glanced across the table as Franco sat there like a statue, staring unblinkingly out the window. His phone buzzed again.

When he didn't move this time, she said, "Franco, it's your phone."

That startled him out of his deep thoughts. As he reached for his phone, she studied him. From his short dark curls on the top of his head to his clean-shaven face to those intense, dark eyes that felt as though they could totally see through her, to his aristocratic nose and finally to those very kissable lips—not that she'd had the luxury of feeling his mouth pressed to hers.

While he rapidly sent some text messages, she continued her leisurely view of the man that she'd just proposed to. He had broad, strong shoulders and a muscular chest. And then there were his hands, with his long, lean fingers. Her mother would have said that he had the hands of a concert pianist—as her mother had been a concert pianist until she'd married. But if Carla were a betting person, she'd say that Franco didn't know the C key from the A.

Franco slipped his phone in his pocket. His gaze met hers. "Sorry. It was business."

She nodded in understanding. "No problem. I know your family business is as important to you as mine is to me."

His eyes lit up. "We do have that in common. But you've obviously misinterpreted our time together—"

"I didn't." Heat rushed to her face as she realized he thought she was in love with him—

nothing could be further from the truth. "I have no illusions about what a marriage between us would be like."

His gaze narrowed in on her. "So you're not in love with me?"

She couldn't hold back the laughter that bubbled up inside her. Sure, he was drop-dead gorgeous, but he had one big fault—he was like her father, always thinking about business. And she had no desire to marry anyone. "Of course not. Is that what you thought?"

He shrugged. "Well, that's usually why people get married."

"But we're not usual people, are we?"

"Even so, I'm not getting married—not to you or anyone else." His tone was firm and unbending.

She wasn't giving up now. "Listen, I know this marriage idea is a bit of a surprise—okay, it's a big shocker—but don't dismiss the idea so quickly. It could be beneficial to both of us."

He didn't say anything for a moment as he continued to stare at her—as though he were trying to break through her barriers and read her most intimate thoughts. Not that she'd let him get that close.

She'd already been hurt enough by her college sweetheart. Matteo had been Mr. Popularity, and she'd been the socialite with all the right connections.

Matteo had been eager to get into politics, and though she saw herself as being more than a politician's wife, she'd agreed to marry him. Her parents had been delighted. And so after graduation, they'd delayed the wedding and instead thrown themselves into Matteo's first campaign.

It had been a grueling year of public events, dinners and interviews. She felt as though the layers of her life had been peeled back for all the world to see.

It wasn't just her life the press had delved into. And that's when they'd exposed Matteo's duplicity. The story of him conducting an affair with his campaign manager was front-page news, complete with a picture of them wrapped up in each other's arms kissing.

Just the memory made her shudder inwardly. She'd barely dodged that disaster. She never wanted to let herself be that vulnerable again.

She gave herself a mental shake, chasing away the troublesome thoughts from the past. She was no longer that doe-eyed girl who thought love would win out. Her heart had been hardened. She was much more practical now.

While Franco might be the most handsome man she'd ever met, she had absolutely no intention of acting upon that chemistry. This would be a business arrangement, nothing more.

His gaze narrowed. "Beneficial how?"

"Should I marry, I assume full control of the

company for six months, during which time my father can't override any of my decisions."

A flicker of interest ignited in his dark eyes. "And what's in it for me?"

"I know you want your products once more on all the tables in the Falco chain. That's a lot of tables—many more than there were back when our families were doing business together."

"And you will have the power to make that happen."

She nodded. "My signed, sealed and official agreement gives me all the power, once I marry."

Franco's brows rose. Her totally outlandish scheme had caught and held his attention. She suppressed a smile that threatened to lift her lips. Now wasn't the time for gloating over a plan that would not only benefit the two of them, but more importantly it'd help her father—even if he was too stubborn to see it.

CHAPTER TWO

MARRIAGE WAS OUT of the question.

It was tantamount to self-destruction.

And yet this proposal was most tempting.

Franco couldn't believe he was not only entertaining the thought of marrying Carla but also very tempted to say yes.

With his appetite long forgotten, he glanced across the table. Carla's unfinished meal had been pushed off to the side. It appeared neither of them were that hungry. He paid the check, and then they headed outside. He had no particular destination in mind.

When he'd accepted her request for this dinner, he figured it would be to turn down his latest business proposal to place his spices back in the Falco Fresco Ristorantes. Carla's family's company was the largest restaurant chain in all of Italy. It spanned from the northern fringes of the country down to the warm shores of Naples. It'd taken decades for the chain to be the most well-known name in Italy, but they'd succeeded.

And Franco liked to think his family had something to do with it, seeing as his family's spices were what they'd used in the restaurant until more recent years.

But why did the success of both of their businesses have to hinge on marriage?

He raked his fingers through his hair as he tried to figure out another solution, one that was amenable to both of them. He stopped walking. He turned to Carla and gazed into her beautiful brown eyes. For a moment, he forgot what he was going to say. Her beauty, well, it was unique, and it didn't come from makeup.

It started with her heart-shaped face, her warm brown eyes and long lashes. She had high cheekbones, a pert nose and lush lips. She was stunning. But he refused to let himself get distracted. This was too important.

He swallowed hard. "Does your agreement with your father state that you have to marry me in order for it to be valid?"

"Of course not. My father hates your family."

He refrained from stating that his grandfather felt the same way about her father. Though he did recall his grandfather's warning that he couldn't trust a Falco. So did Carla have something else in mind besides a business arrangement?

"I propose you marry someone else," he said, though the idea of Carla pledging her heart to someone else didn't appeal to him—not at all. "And then you'll be free to do business with my company."

"I've considered the idea." She hesitated.

"And?"

When her gaze met his, her eyes were shuttered, blocking him out. "And I can't trust anyone else to do this."

"And you think you can trust me? Maybe you should talk to your father about that." He was certain her father would talk her out of this crazy idea.

She stepped up to him. "I can trust you because I know you're totally opposed to marriage."

"And what does that have to do with this?"

"It means that when it comes time to dissolve this partnership, you won't give me a hard time. You won't have developed any illusions that there was something more to this arrangement than what we agree to now."

There was certainly more to Carla than he'd ever imagined. This cool and calculating businesswoman was a side of her that he'd never seen before, and he wasn't quite sure how to react. Part of him respected the fact that she took her family's business so seriously that she'd be willing to go this far to look after it. Luckily he hadn't had to go that far—well, not yet.

He'd worked like crazy over the past several

months, meeting with smaller restaurant chains and grocers, but no satisfactory deals had been reached. His grandfather had made sure to point out his failures. The comments still stung. But Franco was determined to prove to his grandfather that he was a skillful businessman. And now Carla was offering him a prime opportunity to do exactly that, but could he afford her price?

He couldn't believe he was asking this, but stranger things were known to happen. "How long would the marriage have to last?"

"Six months."

Six months. Twenty-six weeks. One hundred and eighty-two days. A lifetime.

As they resumed walking, he forked his fingers through his hair again. The last thing he was worried about at this moment was appearances. He was more worried about breaking the promise he'd made himself when his mother had dumped him and his brother on their grandparents' doorstep—he would never let himself be vulnerable again. And that included marriage—most especially marriage.

But this wasn't a typical marriage. Right?

His sideways glance met Carla's expectant look once more. "And do you promise that if we do this—if we marry—you won't expect anything from me?"

She averted her gaze. "There might be some stipulations."

He knew it! He knew when it came to marriage no one could be trusted. "Forget it." He shook his head. "We aren't doing this."

"Don't you even want to hear the stipulations before you write off my offer?"

Did he have to hear them? She probably wanted weekends together, family gatherings and all the other stuff that people did when they were trying to show the world their marriage wasn't a complete and utter sham. He wasn't doing it.

"No. Forget it."

"Well," she said, "you might not want to hear them, but I'm going to tell you. There will be no stepping out on the marriage. So you'll have to say goodbye to any girlfriends for the length of our marriage. I won't be made a laughingstock."

Hmm…that wasn't so bad. It wasn't like he had a serious girlfriend. Unlike his brother used to do, he did maintain girlfriends for longer than two weeks. But he made it perfectly clear from the beginning that the relationship wouldn't go anywhere. It was all for fun—nothing more.

But the last woman he'd casually dated had been a little scary. So he'd been avoiding dating for the past couple of months. He didn't see how Carla's stipulation would be an issue, especially with a wife like Carla. His gaze lingered on her. They could definitely have some fun together.

"And we will not be consummating the marriage." It was as though she'd read his mind. Was he that obvious about his attraction to her?

"Are you sure that part isn't negotiable?" He sent her a teasing smile.

She glowered at him. Okay, so she was taking this all very seriously. He supposed he should, too, though he didn't want to. No matter the outcome, there was still an integral part of him that was utterly opposed to this arrangement.

He cleared his throat. "Sorry. I guess I'm just really having a hard time taking this seriously."

"Don't I look serious enough for you?" Her unwavering gaze met his.

"It's not that. You definitely act as though you're negotiating the most important deal of your life."

"Then what's the problem? I thought this deal would give you exactly what you wanted."

He rubbed the back of his neck. "It's the marriage part that I'm having problems with. Couldn't we just fake the marriage like my brother and your cousin did with their engagement?"

"It has to be a real marriage, otherwise I won't assume control of the company and I won't be able to hammer out a mutually beneficial arrangement to put your products back in my family's restaurants. But this time around, I'm foreseeing a much bigger tie-in and promotion."

She certainly knew how to sweet-talk him.

But still, he'd promised himself not to marry—
not to make the same mistakes as his parents.
He knew a secret about their marriage—a secret that his brother didn't know—a secret he
wasn't supposed to know.

His conception had been a mistake. That's
how his father had put it in an argument with
his mother. He was the mistake that kept them
married longer than they'd wanted. If it wasn't
for his presence, his parents would have gone
their separate ways without destroying the child-
hoods of both him and his brother.

And though the logical part of his brain said
that none of it was his fault, the other part of him
felt bad that his mere existence had caused his
brother so much harm, from their father walking out on them to their broken home to their
mother abandoning them on their grandparents'
doorstep.

But if he didn't do this—if he didn't agree to
marry Carla—how much more damage would
be done? Because those products that were in
danger of being pulled out of production weren't
just from the company's past. They were the future of the company.

The company's sales had slumped over the
years. Younger buyers weren't recognizing the
Marchello name. They weren't rushing to the
grocers to buy their product, so it was just a

matter of time until their company became extinct. Did he really have a choice in the matter?

"Wait." Carla's voice drew him from his intense thoughts. They paused along a quiet stretch of sidewalk. When his gaze focused on her, he saw her withdraw folded papers from her purse. "This should explain the details of the agreement."

He was a little dumbfounded that she would have a legal agreement already drawn up. Surely he'd misunderstood. But when he wordlessly took the papers from her, he saw her name at the top followed by his.

He was shocked that she would think he would just readily agree to such an outlandish idea. After all, he wasn't an author, like his younger brother, and eager to live out a fictional life.

But he was also impressed with Carla's get-it-done attitude. It said a lot about her. It also told him that they had a lot in common. Was it something they could build upon? Not as in building a real marriage, but a real business relationship. Something told him that this deal, though it went against everything he'd ever promised himself, was too good to pass up.

And besides, it would be a marriage on paper only. Soon it would be over—though not soon enough.

He glanced down over the top sheet, catching

the important details: their names; the length of marriage; the agreement to display, use and serve Marchello spices in all Falco Fresco Ristorantes.

"Okay." He folded the papers. "I'll have my attorney go over these. Then we can sign the papers and set a date for the—well, you know."

"The wedding. I had a thought about that, too."

Why was he not surprised? It appeared she had thought about everything. He wondered if this was a sign of how things would go with their m…arrangement.

He cleared his throat. "And what would that be?"

"I think we need to get moving on this. We can get married at the same time we sign the papers."

"That soon?" His throat grew tight, and it was getting hard to breathe.

"Is there a reason we should put things off?"

Other than to give him more time to get used to the idea—which was never, ever going to happen—nothing stood in their way.

When his gaze met hers, he saw the worry reflected in her eyes. It was now, as the initial shock subsided, that he noticed the shadows beneath her eyes and the lines bracketing her mouth. Though she might be proposing this plan, it didn't appear it had been by choice but rather one of self-preservation.

"If you aren't interested in the deal, I'll find someone else."

She didn't say it, but he filled in the blank— she could easily find another willing participant. And if she were to do that, he was certain the door would be firmly closed on ever getting his products back in the Falcos' restaurants.

"I'll do it." Once the words passed his lips, he felt as though he'd just shackled himself to Carla.

He gave her a quick glance, from her long dark hair to her warm brown eyes down to her pouty lips that were just begging to be kissed. Okay, so there were much worse people to be chained to.

"Good." She glanced around as though trying to determine where their meandering had led them. "Perhaps we should turn around." When he nodded in compliance, she said, "Have your attorney look over the contract, and we'll set the date to finalize everything."

"Don't you mean set our wedding date?" He couldn't resist pointing out the obvious.

Color flared in her cheeks. "Yes, that, too."

So she wasn't any more eager than he was to exchange wedding vows. But it wasn't going to be that easy.

"I have some demands, too," he said.

Carla's eyes momentarily widened with surprise before she returned to her neutral expression. In a practically monotone voice she asked, "What would those be?"

"We need to move immediately on getting Marchello Spices back in the restaurants."

She nodded. "I knew you'd expect nothing less. It'll be our first order of business."

"I have other ideas—"

"I'm sure you do, but don't get ahead of yourself."

"But I won't sign unless it's in writing about Marchello Spices being returned to tables immediately."

As they continued their stroll, Carla didn't say anything at first. In her beautiful eyes, he could see the wheels of her mind turning. Surely she had to see the merits of this plan. It would breathe new life into the restaurant chain. It would benefit both of their companies.

"Have your attorneys write up an addendum to the current agreement and I'll have my people go over it."

He stopped next to her small yellow sports car. "I'll do that."

"Remember, time is of the essence."

"This will be my top priority." He opened the car door for her. "Are you really sure you want to do this? This agreement is quite unprecedented."

Her unwavering gaze met his. "Sometimes sacrifices have to be made. It is a marriage in name only. And it is only six months. But it has to look convincing. My father has to believe this is a real, traditional marriage. Anything less and he'll have us tied up in litigation."

He sighed. "Agreed."

"So how do we get him to the wedding without him knowing that he's going to our wedding? Because he'll need to see it with his own eyes if he's to believe it." She paused as though giving the dilemma some serious thought.

Franco gave it some thought. "I know. We'll invite everyone to a special event—a special announcement."

Her eyes lit up with interest. "I like the way you think."

"Just remember, this was all your idea."

"How could I forget? But it'll be worth it in the end. Everyone will get what they want or need."

He nodded in understanding. It wasn't until he was seated in his own car that he realized he'd been holding his breath. Perhaps because he'd been holding back an argument—this was too much of a sacrifice for business.

Wait. Had he just thought that? He was the one who was all business, all the time. But this marriage contract felt over-the-top even for him.

What if Carla changed her mind about what

she wanted from this marriage? Then he recalled her cold and businesslike demeanor during their dinner. She was no longer the fun and vivacious young woman that he'd met at his sister-in-law's villa not so long ago. Something had changed in her—something he couldn't identify.

And when it came down to it, her offer was just too good to pass up.

But could he really utter the words *I do*?

CHAPTER THREE

THERE WAS A diamond ring in his pocket.

It felt as though it were burning a hole through his slacks.

Franco thought back to when his grandmother had given him the ring, the same evening she'd given his brother an heirloom ring to properly propose to his now wife, Gianna. His grandmother had told Franco that she was giving him the ring, even though he wasn't involved with anyone, because he was the type to play things close to his chest. And she doubted when the time came to propose that he'd come to her for the ring.

He'd tried vehemently to refuse it, but what can you do when your grandmother gives you that look? You know, the one where her face turns serious, a brow is arched over the rim of her glasses and the look in her eyes says *if you don't do what I say, you're going to live to regret it*? Yeah, that one. Well, that's exactly what she'd done to him. And the last thing he'd wanted to do was have his grandmother upset with him. Because he loved his grandmother dearly—she was the only true mother figure in his life. She never wavered—never shrank away. She was calm and she was steady.

So when Carla sounded frantic about making time for her father, attending to business at the office and preparing for the quarterly board meeting, he'd offered to have his assistant send out invitations to a private party where a big announcement was to be made as well as throw together an intimate wedding. Carla had sounded so relieved when she'd accepted his offer. And that was why he had a diamond ring readily available when his assistant had asked about Carla's engagement ring. It was the one detail he needed to take care of personally.

Still, this wedding was so much more involved than he'd been prepared for when he'd first agreed to the marriage contract. He'd thought they'd exchange empty vows and then coexist for six months. Instead, they needed a real wedding with select guests and a photographer. He'd had no idea their arrangement would go to these lengths in order to sell it to her father. But Franco didn't want to leave anything up to chance.

Today was their wedding day. Franco's gut was tied in a knot. He hadn't eaten a thing since yesterday. Not even coffee appealed to him. He wondered if all grooms felt this anxious.

He pulled to a stop in a no-parking zone, right in front of Carla's apartment building. He couldn't back out now. He just had to get through the day the best he could.

Franco exited the car at the same time she stepped onto the sidewalk. She rushed up to him with her overnight bag in hand. Her face was pale, but that was the only clue she was nervous.

"Are you ready for this?"

"As ready as I'm ever going to be. My father wasn't happy about the mysterious party, but I talked him into going. What about your grandparents?"

"They're out of the country."

"Oh."

He didn't like her disapproving tone. "What's the matter?"

She shook her head. "Nothing."

When she moved to walk past him, he stepped in her way. "If we're going to marry, you have to learn to talk to me."

She glanced away. "I just wondered if getting married without your grandparents—well, if it would bother you."

"If this was a real wedding, yes, it would. But since this is a business arrangement, I can live with it. In fact, it'll be easier this way. Besides, it's probably best my grandfather and your father aren't in close proximity."

She nodded in agreement.

He took her bag and stowed it in the boot of the car before they set off on their journey. The fact of the matter was he had a surprise in store for Carla. He hoped she'd like it.

"Where are we going?" she asked as they headed away from the center of Verona. "I thought we'd have a quick wedding in the city."

"You'll soon see."

She turned to him. Her expression was very serious. "We don't have time for distractions. We have to get the papers signed and then we have to get straight to work. I have to let my key people know that we're shifting gears and focusing full-time on our collaboration."

"That can wait for a day."

"No, it can't—"

"Yes, it can." He could hardly believe he was saying these words. And all this time his family had accused him of being a workaholic. Obviously they didn't know Carla very well, or they might realize that she definitely outdid him.

"Franco, if we're going to make this all work out in time, we can't waste a moment."

"But for any of it to work, we must marry—"

"Quickly and without fuss—"

"Aw…but you forget that your father needs to believe in this marriage—a marriage to a

Marchello. You know as well as I do that he's going to fight this marriage. If we aren't careful, he'll prove us frauds, and then our agreement will be null and void."

Her mouth opened. No words came out. Then she pressed her lips together with a deep sigh. "Fine. What do you have in mind?"

"You'll see. Trust me."

"That's the problem," she said. "I don't trust you."

He let out a laugh. The truth was that he didn't trust her, either. It definitely wasn't the correct way to start a marriage. But then again, this was a business partnership. And when it came to business agreements, there was always a bit of distrust. So the way he saw it, they were okay with this. But as they headed out of the city, he realized there was one other thing they needed to deal with sooner rather than later.

He swallowed hard. "There's something else we need to do to seal the deal."

Carla turned to him with concern reflected in her eyes. "Do I even want to ask what you're referring to? Because if this is about consummating our marriage—"

"It's not, I assure you." Though that's one part of the day that might be quite enjoyable. As soon as the thought came to him, he dismissed it. Blurring lines between business and pleasure was never a good idea.

He pulled off to the side of the road. He reached in his pocket and pulled out the ring. There was a distinct gasp from Carla. He glanced at her, but she wasn't looking at him. Her full attention was focused on the ring in his hand.

"If we are going to do this right—" his voice wobbled, at least to his ears "—we need to be properly engaged. So… Carla Falco, will you marry me?"

Her gaze flickered to meet his. He could see the wheels of her mind spinning. He hadn't thought this would catch her so off guard. Didn't all women look forward to receiving a diamond ring? Her gaze moved back to the ring, but she didn't reach for it.

"Go ahead. Take it." He moved it closer to her. "It won't bite you. I promise." When she still didn't reach for it, he said, "You know you have to play the part, just like I do."

At last she took the ring from him and slipped it on her finger. "I guess you're right." She held up her hand, letting the light twinkle off the diamond. "It's very pretty."

"It was my great-grandmother's ring."

"Oh." She quickly pulled it off and handed it back to him. "I can't accept this, even on a temporary basis."

"I want you to wear it." And then realizing how that might sound, he clarified himself. "I mean my grandmother expects my wife to wear the ring. If you don't, everyone will wonder why you don't have it on. Do you really want to answer those questions?"

"No. I suppose not." She placed the ring back on her finger. "But it's going to make me very nervous. What if I damage it?"

"You won't."

"But I might."

"It'll be okay because I have no intention of using the ring for a real marriage, so no one will know."

"I'll know."

They continued to ride on quietly, each lost in their own thoughts. What had sounded like a good idea at one point—a means to an end— was now sounding so much more involved with so many entanglements. He couldn't help but wonder what details he'd forgotten about for this big day. He'd just have to hope they wouldn't be big enough to be noticed by anyone—including their families.

It had been a week of negotiations.

A week of hammering out the details of their future.

If Carla had any doubts about proposing a marriage between herself and Franco, those doubts were quickly quelled. Nothing about this upcoming marriage felt personal in the least. Her gaze strayed to the heirloom diamond ring on her finger. Okay, maybe it was a little personal.

The thought that her father's reckless disregard for his own health had pushed her to this drastic decision hadn't gone unnoticed. Though she was very upset with him, her concern about his teetering health trumped everything. And so she would go through with this crazy plan.

She leaned back against the buttery-soft black leather of the chauffeured sedan. She glanced over to Franco. A large gap yawned between them. She took comfort in knowing that he wasn't any more anxious for this union.

And though when they'd first met she'd thought he was attracted to her, she now realized it must have all been in her imagination. Because ever since she'd proposed to him, he'd kept a respectable distance from her.

This was going to work out just the way she'd planned. Still, the thought of a loveless marriage left her saddened. Call it the romantic in her or maybe she'd read one too many romance novels, but she'd been under the illusion that marriage was supposed to be about love. Nothing could be further from the truth where they were concerned.

But without emotional entanglements, she'd be able to focus her full attention on the family business. That was what she wanted after all. She just had to keep that in mind.

Carla turned her attention back to the passing scenery. "Where are we going?"

"You'll like this. Just relax," Franco said.

Carla sighed. The truth was she couldn't relax. She'd barely slept a wink the night before. She'd watched infomercials, thinking they'd bore her to sleep. No such luck. She'd tried chamomile tea. Nothing. At last, she'd lain in the dark, tossing and turning. Sometime in the middle of the night, she'd nodded off. She wondered if all brides were this nervous.

Not that this was a real wedding. It wasn't like she had feelings for Franco. Though he was gorgeous. He was so serious most of the time.

She chanced a glance at Franco. He was staring out the window. And then he consulted his Rolex. He was probably wondering how soon this wedding would be over so he could get on with his business.

But what would he be like if he were marrying for love? Would his sole focus be on his bride? Would he be able to think of anything else but spending every waking moment with his beloved? An uneasy feeling churned in the pit of her stomach.

She let out a soft sigh and turned away. It wasn't like she wanted him to look at her that way. She knew how fleeting love could be. And when things fell apart, it was messy and painful. She refused to set herself up to be hurt again.

Just outside the small village of Gemma, where her cousin lived, the car slowed and turned into a short drive. It led them up to a stately house that sat right on the edge of Lake Como. The house appeared to be three stories with tall windows. She didn't recognize it.

She turned to Franco. "What are we doing here?"

"I thought it'd be a good place to have a wedding."

As the car pulled around to the front of the villa, she caught a quick glimpse of the lush garden bordering the lake. Her attention turned to the impressive villa. It had floor-to-ceiling windows, allowing a picturesque view of the lake.

Whoever owned this villa was most fortunate. She couldn't even imagine how much a house in this stunning setting would cost. Though she'd always thought her father had the most beautiful house in the Lake Como region, she had to admit that this house definitely rivaled it. No, it surpassed it in size, location and sheer beauty. What a place for a wedding.

"Who owns this place?" Carla asked.

"I do. Now that my brother lives here, I wanted to have a place close by."

"It's beautiful."

Standing off to the side of the driveway was a stylish young woman with a digital notepad clutched in her arm. A smile lit up her face as she looked expectantly at Carla. Who was she? Carla glanced over at Franco, waiting for some sort of explanation.

"Go ahead," he said. "Everything is waiting for you."

"Everything?" She didn't know what to expect.

He lowered his voice so as not to be overheard. "We both know this has to look real or else your father isn't going to believe it."

She opened her mouth to argue but then wordlessly closed it. As much as she hated it, Franco was right.

"I've seen to all the details, including a few guests as well as my brother and your cousin."

"You invited them, too?" she whispered. "But why? Couldn't you have just invited people from your office?"

"You do want people to believe this marriage is real, right? Isn't that the only way your agreement with your father will be ironclad?"

"Yes, but…" Her frantic thoughts were fragmented. "This…it feels wrong. We invited everyone under false pretenses."

"You don't think they'll be excited by the surprise wedding?"

She frowned at him. "That's not what I mean. They'll assume that you and I…that we're…"

"In love? I know." His hushed tone was matter-of-fact.

"And it doesn't bother you?"

He shrugged. "I guess I'm just used to people making assumptions about me."

This stirred her interest. "What sort of assumptions?"

This time he glanced away. "All sorts of things. That I'm a bloodthirsty businessman. That I ran off my father so I could assume the CEO position."

"But that's ridiculous. He left when you were just a little kid." When Franco's surprised gaze turned her way, she realized she'd overstepped. "I'm sorry. My cousin told me a little of Dario's background, which is also your background."

Understanding flashed in his eyes. "Anyway, people are going to think what they want, but in the end, I think our families will understand that we did what we thought was best for everyone."

She had her doubts. "I really hope you're right."

He reached out and gave her hand a quick squeeze. "It's going to be okay."

She wanted to believe him. This was her one chance to get her stubborn father to do the right thing—hand over the reins to the company so he could get his strength back. And whether she wanted to admit it or not, it was the right thing for her, too.

Her gaze searched his. She'd had no idea Franco would go to these lengths. But why shouldn't he? He had a lot riding on this wedding. The entire future of his company was on the line.

"I don't know if I can do this," she whispered.

"Sure, you can. Everything is in motion. All you have to do is act like the loving fiancée."

"Everyone thinks we're in love?" When he nodded, she asked, "Even your assistant?"

"Most especially her."

"Why?"

"Because she is our front person. She has to legitimately be able to sell our whirlwind love story to the guests."

"You mean my father?"

He nodded once more. "I don't think your father is going to be happy about you marrying a Marchello."

"No, he won't. He wasn't happy when my cousin married your brother. He'll be furious about our marriage."

"But your agreement with him didn't say whom you had to marry, so we're good." His gaze searched hers. "Do you think you'll be able to pull this off?"

Part of her said that it was too much, but the other part of her—the business part of her—said she could do this if it meant saving her father from himself.

"Yes." Her answer was soft but firm, even if all the while her stomach roiled with nerves.

"Relax. It's all been arranged. I'll see you shortly." And with that he walked away with an older woman who wore a dark skirt suit with her dark hair pulled up in a bun.

Carla wasn't sure what to expect. When she'd initially broached the subject of marriage, she'd expected something quick, efficient and businesslike. But this lakeside villa was so far from anything she'd had in mind. This was the setting for a real wedding. Not what they were about to do.

Still, as the young woman continued to stare at her with that plastered-on smile, Carla had no choice but to step out of the car and find out what Franco had in store for her.

Carla approached the young woman. "Hello. I'm Carla Falco."

"Oh, I know who you are. I've seen your photo on the internet. It's an honor to meet you." The young woman's face filled with color. "I can't believe I got to plan your wedding. We better hurry inside before the guests begin to arrive." The young woman set off down the stone walk toward the large double doors of the villa.

It was true. Carla was in the news quite often, as she sat on many charity boards. And lately, her father's health scare had propelled them into the headlines. The public had a vested interest in the welfare of Falco's Fresco Ristorantes.

What in the world had Franco planned? It really seemed like a lot of trouble for a fake wedding. Well, it would be real on paper, but still, it wasn't like they were in love or anything. But she had to admit that her curiosity was piqued, and so she followed along.

CHAPTER FOUR

"What are you doing?"

It was the same question Franco had been asking himself ever since he'd agreed to Carla's absolutely off-the-wall idea. And what made him think a brief marriage—a marriage based on a mutually beneficial business arrangement—would end any better than his parents' painful and disastrous divorce?

His gaze focused on his younger brother, Dario. There was expectation on his face. If he couldn't get his brother to believe in this marriage, what chance did he have of convincing anyone else? Still, he had to do his best.

Franco raked his fingers through his hair. "I'm getting married."

Dario moved to stand in front of him. His gaze searched his face. "You don't look like a man anxious to walk down the aisle."

Franco attempted a reassuring smile, but catching his reflection in the mirror, he realized his smile ended up as some distorted look that was more a frown than a look of happiness. He glanced away. "It...it's complicated."

"She's pregnant, too?" Dario's eyes widened.

"No!" Franco's voice thundered through the room. He swallowed hard and then lowered his voice. "Wait. You said *too*." It took him a second to string his thoughts together. "Are you saying Gianna is pregnant?"

Dario smiled and seemed to stand a bit taller. "She is."

"Congrats!" Franco hugged his younger brother and clapped him on the back. "That's awesome."

"Thanks. It is pretty great." Dario wore a big, happy grin. But then he sobered up. "But we're talking about you and Carla. Are you sure—"

"I'm sure she's not pregnant. You know I wouldn't let that happen."

Relief reflected in Dario's eyes. "I should have known after what you went through with Rose that you would be extra cautious. But sometimes things happen."

Franco tried to block Rose from his thoughts, because every time he thought of her, he once again grew angry at her deception. Rose had lied to him about being pregnant, knowing he could never turn his back on a child of his own. In the end, it'd all been a ploy to get him to marry her. And after a fake pregnancy test, she'd almost snared him into a loveless marriage. But when he'd insisted on a second test with his doctor, the truth came tumbling out.

"Carla is nothing at all like Rose," he ground out.

"I didn't mean to imply that she was."

"Good." Franco began to pace the floor, feeling like a caged animal.

"I'm no expert on marriage, even if I am married. But I'm just going to put this out there—marrying the woman you love shouldn't be complicated. It should be all about you and her and being anxious to share your life with her."

Franco's head snapped back around to look at his brother. "I can't believe you said that. I thought you were the one who was totally opposed to marriage."

Dario shrugged. "What can I say? Gianna changed my mind."

"Apparently. But what you two have, well, it isn't the same with Carla and me."

Dario's dark brows furrowed together. "How is it, then?"

Franco hesitated. It was on the tip of his tongue to tell his brother everything. But then he recalled promising Carla that he'd keep this all to himself. It was the only way this was going to work.

"It's just nerves." Franco's tone was firm.

Dario reached out and gripped Franco's shoulders. "Listen, if you aren't sure, back out now. It'll be best for the both of you—"

"No. This is what's best." He pulled free from his brother's hold. He turned away from Dario's concerned look. It's what was best for his family's future. It's what was best for Carla's very stubborn father. It's what was best for their respective businesses. "Trust me."

Silence filled the room, and for a moment all Franco could hear was the pounding of his heart echoing in his ears. In all his life, he never imagined that he'd be standing in this position. Today was his wedding day—a wedding to a woman he didn't love and who didn't love him.

And then that last thought struck him. He was worked up over nothing. If they weren't emotionally invested in this union, there's no way they could get hurt. There was nothing to worry about. Nothing at all—

"This isn't right," Dario said. "You need to take more time to think this marriage over."

"This from the man who faked his own engagement." Now when he spoke his voice was calmer, more certain.

"That was different."

"Was it?" This time it was Franco nailing his little brother with an inquisitive stare. "As I recall, you came up with your fake engagement spontaneously."

Dario's gaze narrowed. "I had to do it. You

and the family wouldn't have left me alone to finish the book otherwise, and…and Gianna had her own reasons to go along with it."

"Yet it all worked out in the end." He was truly happy for his brother. And though Dario had found his own true love, that didn't mean Franco would find his.

"But that is different," Dario said. "Gianna and I had time to get to know each other really well before we said *I do*. How much do you know about Carla?"

He hadn't been expecting a pop quiz. "I know that when she smiles, the whole world lights up." That was no lie. "I know she's had a lot on her shoulders with her father's failing health." He paused as he drew on his memories. "I know that she prefers capellini to spaghetti. I know she loves wine but not scotch." His gaze searched his brothers. "What else do you want to know? How she likes to be kissed?"

Dario's face scrunched up in a look of disgust. "Ugh! No. You can keep those details to yourself."

"Good." A smug smile came over Franco's face at his ability to quiet his brother.

The truth of the matter was that Franco had yet to figure out how he could kiss her and not mess up their very delicate working relationship. But that didn't mean he hadn't been curious about how her full, luscious lips would feel beneath his.

"You're sure about this?" Dario asked one last time.

"I am. I know exactly what I'm getting myself into."

And now that he realized not loving his wife meant that he was protected from any pain when the marriage ended, he just had to keep up the barrier between them.

As for the kiss that he'd been wondering about, well, he would just have to go on wondering. Because he knew that a single kiss with Carla wouldn't just be a single kiss. It would lead to another kiss and another one until things totally spiraled out of control. And where would that leave them?

He gave himself a mental shake. It would be best just to avoid the whole thing. No kissing. No spiraling out of control. And definitely no falling for beautiful, enticing Carla.

This all felt so unreal.

Today was her wedding day.

Carla didn't care how many deep slow breaths she breathed in and blew out or how many times she assured herself that this was only a business arrangement, she couldn't settle her wildly beating heart. She'd negotiated million-dollar deals—deals that could have crippled her company—and she'd been able to handle them calmly and coolly. Why couldn't she do that now?

As she followed Franco's assistant, Mia, through the entrance of the stately villa, she felt as though this whole day was some sort of out-of-body experience. She frantically went over all her options—they were few. In the end, she came back to the same conclusion that she'd come to when she'd masterminded this totally outrageous plan.

They made their way up a set of sweeping steps to the second story. At the end of a very short hallway was a dark wooden door. Mia opened it and stood aside for Carla to enter. When she stepped into the spacious and warmly decorated room, she found she wasn't alone. Her cousin Gianna was standing out on the small balcony.

Gianna turned and rushed inside. "We need to talk."

"What's wrong?" Was it her father? Her heart raced. Had something happened to him?

Gianna smiled. "Relax. It's good news. But I can't wait any longer to tell you."

"Well, tell me."

"I'm pregnant." Gianna's whole face glowed with happiness.

"That's wonderful!" Carla hugged her cousin. When she pulled back, she said, "Congratulations. I'm going to be, what? A second cousin? Or is it first cousin once removed? That always confuses me."

"I don't know about that, but as soon as we get you married, you'll be the baby's aunt." Gianna continued to smile at her like the wedding was the best thing in the world.

Carla swallowed hard as she forced a smile to her face. If only her cousin knew the truth about the wedding, she wouldn't be so happy. "This is a day for lots of celebrating." Carla turned to Mia. "Thank you so much for everything. But we've got it from here."

Mia nodded. "But before I go, I wanted to show you what Franco ordered for you."

"Ordered for me?"

Mia smiled and nodded. And then she showed both women the rack of wedding gowns and maid of honor dresses. There were accessories to choose from. And there were even flowers in her favorite color—plum.

After they thanked Mia for all her help, Franco's assistant left them alone to go check on the groom. Carla wanted to dislike the woman, who was Franco's right hand, but she couldn't. Mia was one of those people who was genuinely nice.

And though Mia spoke highly of her boss,

she was also engaged to a man who made her eyes twinkle with love when she mentioned him. Besides, it wasn't like Carla had any hold over Franco. Sure, they were going to be married, and yes, they'd agreed to be faithful to each other, but that didn't mean they would have a traditional marriage—a marriage like her parents'.

Immediately, her eyes blurred with unshed tears. In that moment, she realized what was really bothering her—her mother wasn't here to share this day with her. She'd always thought as a young girl that her beloved mother would be next to her as she reached the major milestones in her life.

Her mother's absence left a gaping hole in her heart that time hadn't sufficiently healed. As her gaze moved across the rack of stunning dresses, she realized she'd always thought she'd be trying them on with her mother looking on, helping to choose the right one.

Now she was about to marry a man she didn't love in order to protect her father from an early grave. And her mother wasn't there to calm her rising nerves. Nothing about this was right.

Tears dropped onto her cheeks.

"Are you all right?" Gianna moved to her side.

Carla swiped away the tears. "I'm fine. It's just a lot. And…and I wish my mother was here to share this day with me."

Gianna hugged her. "She's here. She wouldn't miss it."

Carla pulled back and nodded. "I know. It's just not the same."

And if she was looking on, would she understand her daughter's choices? Would she understand how her abrupt absence had made Carla desperate to keep her father in her life as long as possible?

Gianna turned to Carla. "And you have me. I'll always be there for you. But why didn't you tell me?"

At first, Carla thought her cousin knew about the marriage contract, and then she realized that was impossible. Other than the army of attorneys, who weren't allowed to speak of it, only three people knew of the marriage contract: her father, Franco and herself. And she was quite certain none of them would speak of it. She knew her father was too proud a man to tell people that he'd been cornered into an agreement to hand over the reins of his company to his daughter in order to get her to marry.

"You mean about the marriage?" Carla moved to the rack of hangers with white garment bags hanging from it.

"Of course the marriage." Gianna looked at her with an I-can't-believe-you look. "It…it's all so sudden."

"Once we knew what we wanted, we didn't want to wait."

Gianna nodded in understanding. "Does your father know you're marrying a Marchello?"

"Not exactly." Carla lowered her gaze. "You know how he feels about the Marchellos. If he knew ahead of time, he'd do whatever he could to stop it."

"I'm so sorry. But he'll learn to like Franco. He's a good guy, just like his brother." Gianna held out her hand. "Let me see the ring."

Carla turned and held out her hand with a ring that was quite unlike the style of ring she would have expected from Franco. Somehow she'd expected something big and flashy from him. Instead this ring was smaller and modest. It was exactly what she would have selected for herself.

The fact that it was an heirloom piece she still found surprising. Why would he give her something so meaningful? You only gave rings that had been handed down through the family to people you loved. And they did not love each other. Of that she was certain.

Gianna oohed and aahed over it, making Carla feel increasingly uncomfortable.

"Gianna, there's something I need to tell you—"

"I know. We have to get a move on. We don't want the bride late for the wedding."

At that moment, she recalled her agreement

with Franco to keep the real reason for the marriage to themselves. It was the only chance their marriage contract would hold up under her father's scrutiny. And she wasn't kidding herself into believing that her father wouldn't fight this marriage. But he had no grounds to win, because they were truly going to be husband and wife. The acknowledgment swept the breath from her lungs.

"Carla, are you all right?" Gianna stared at her with worry reflected in her eyes. "You suddenly look pale."

"I, uh—" She struggled to string two words together. "I just need some water. It's a bit warm in here."

Gianna hesitated as though she were going to press the point, but then she kindly moved away to retrieve a glass of water.

Carla knew she had to get a grip on her nerves. This marriage was in the best interests of everyone, including her stubborn father—most especially her father. If it wasn't for him and his risky behavior, she wouldn't even be considering getting married at this stage in her life.

She told herself that everything was going to be all right. She just had to get through today and then life would return to normal. With the marriage behind them, she'd be able to focus on business instead of constantly worrying that her father was overdoing it.

Yes, that's what she'd focus on as she looked through the selection of wedding dresses. This was just a job. Nothing more. She just had to stay focused on the end result—her father would be able to retire and feel reassured that his beloved company was in her safe hands.

CHAPTER FIVE

IT WASN'T TOO LATE.

There was still time to escape.

Franco wore a crisp white shirt and black tie with his tux as he stood by the lakeside, waiting for his bride. *His bride.* The words echoed in his mind as his palms grew damp and his stomach churned. His gaze strayed to the car sitting off to the side of the villa. All he had to do was jump inside and head for freedom. But his feet felt as though they'd been cast in cement.

Part of his mind said that this was the price he'd have to pay to prove to his grandfather and everyone else at the company that he was capable and willing to fully step into the CEO role. He couldn't let a marriage certificate chase him away from fulfilling his dream because he had heard his grandfather mutter something about selling the company.

Running Marchello Spices had been all he could think of since he was young. Perhaps it was a goal that distracted him from the fact that he rarely saw his mother, who was always off with a new husband spending time at the beach in some far-flung country. Or the fact that his father was never around. It was so much easier to focus on something that was more in his control.

And so as a child he'd accompanied his grandfather to the office as often as he would allow him. Franco recalled what it was like being able to go into the CEO's office. And then when he'd been able to sit in his grandfather's seat, he thought he was such big stuff.

He'd wanted to be just like his grandfather when he grew up. He wanted to run the family business and make his grandfather proud of him. And now it was all at his fingertips.

He just had to get through these next few minutes. He'd swear his knees were shaking. He'd glance down and check, but he was frozen in place. He'd never been more nervous in his life. He couldn't imagine what he'd be like if this was a real wedding with real expectations of abiding love for now and forever.

Cold fingertips of apprehension worked their way down his spine. His heart began to beat wildly. His breathing came in one shallow gasp after the other. Was he having a heart attack? Yes, that must be it. He tugged at his too-tight shirt collar. He was certain of it.

He shouldn't do this.

He *couldn't* do this.

"Ladies and gentlemen, gather round," Dario said. "You've all been invited here for a surprise wedding."

There was a round of oohs and aahs.

And then the wedding music began to play. This was his last moment to escape a marriage that would cause nothing but pain to both of them. Or stand here and solidify his company. His mind told him to leave—quickly. There had to be another way—a better way—to keep the business intact and not to lose his seat as CEO.

And then Carla stepped onto the patio. In slow, measured steps, she headed toward him. Her steady gaze met and held his. The longer he stared into her eyes, the calmer he felt. His breathing slowed, and his heartbeat resumed its normal rhythm.

Carlo Falco stepped in front of his daughter, impeding her progress. Oh boy, what was going to happen next? The breath stilled in Franco's lungs as he watched.

"You aren't going to marry *him*." Carlo gave the word *him* an offensive sound.

"I am." Carla's voice was firm.

Franco inwardly cheered her on.

Still, Carlo didn't move as father and daughter continued to glare at each other.

Franco loudly cleared his throat, hoping to distract them from the inevitable argument. It appeared to work when Carla stepped around her father.

Her gaze reconnected with Franco's as she approached him. He wanted to tell her how proud he was of her for standing up to her father. He knew it couldn't have been easy for her.

Franco sent her a reassuring smile, because suddenly this wasn't all about him and what he was risking. It was about helping Carla break free of the hold her father appeared to have over her.

And as long as Carla was by his side, he could get through this—they'd do it together. Finally, he was able to think clearly. He took a moment to really look at his bride. She stole his breath. She wore a long lacy gown that gave a peek at her crystal-studded heels. The gown gathered around her slender waist.

The fitted bodice was decorated with crystals that sparkled in the sunlight. It was held up by two thin straps. Her hair had been pulled up and studded with little white flowers.

But it was the smile on her beautiful face that pulled it all together. She was smiling directly at him. It filled his chest with warmth and a feeling he'd never experienced before.

She couldn't believe she was still walking.

Her knees felt like gelatin, and her ankles were wobbly.

Carla's heart had launched into her throat when her father had stepped in front of her. Anger had flashed in his eyes. She'd thought for sure he was going to make a scene, but then someone had cleared their throat as though reminding them that they had an avid audience. Her father may have refrained from making a public scene, but she knew it wasn't over.

She pushed thoughts of her father to the back of her mind as she continued marching toward her destiny. This really felt like a genuine wedding. It definitely wasn't the simple legal arrangement she'd envisioned. Franco had arranged for a truly authentic wedding including a white lace wedding gown. Oh, and let's not forget the flowers. They were gorgeous plum and blush peonies with greenery to accent the bouquet.

With all the attention to detail that had been put into the day, she was beginning to think there was a whole other side to her soon-to-be husband than she'd originally imagined. The next several months might not be the utter drudgery she'd been imagining.

When she neared her intended groom, she noticed that he cleaned up quite well. He wore a black tux with a black necktie and a crisp white shirt. It looked very sharp on him. He'd shaved, and his hair was still damp from a shower.

She could scarcely believe this was really

happening—a wedding born out of desperation for the two things she loved most—her beloved father and the restaurants where she'd spent so much of her childhood. Because if she didn't make this big sacrifice today, there was a great possibility she'd lose both of them. And that couldn't happen—she wouldn't let it happen.

The longer she stared into Franco's dark, mesmerizing eyes, the more solid her steps became. This was going to work out. She'd picked the right partner. Franco wanted this business deal to succeed as much as she did.

As for that rap-a-tapping of her heart, well, that was just nerves. Pure and simple. Because there was no way the best man from her cousin's wedding had gotten past the carefully laid wall around her tattered heart.

She'd already let one man get close, only to find that she couldn't trust him, and he'd shattered more than just her heart—he'd stolen away her trust, not only in men but in her own judgment. But she wouldn't have that problem with Franco. Her heart wouldn't be on the line.

She continued toward him. She was almost there. She could feel his unease with this whole arrangement. She could totally sympathize.

Just a little longer. Soon it will be over.

And then she stopped in front of him. Could he hear the pounding of her heart?

"Join hands," the minister said.

Before she could utter a word, Franco took her hands in his own. It was only once his steady grip held her fingers that she noticed the slight tremor in her hands. Okay, so she was a little more nervous than she'd been willing to admit.

And then the minister started a traditional service. There was way too much reference to love going on—way too much. She felt like a total fraud. She needed to do something—say something. If the minister kept talking about how their lives would forever be intertwined, she was never going to make it through the wedding.

Before she could utter a word, Franco leaned over and whispered to the minister, "Could we just skip to the important part?"

The minister sent him a knowing smile, as though this wasn't the first time a couple had been anxious to rush to vows. Only Carla was certain the other couples' haste hadn't been because the mention of love and forever while marrying someone they weren't romantically linked with made them uncomfortable.

"Do you, Franco Giuseppe Marchello, take Carla Elana Falco to be your wife?"

There was a pause. Carla's gaze rose to meet his. She immediately saw his indecision. *No. No. We've come too far for you to back out now.*

"Franco," prompted the minister.

Her gaze flickered to the minister, whose attention was fully focused on her intended. She turned back to Franco. His gaze was downcast. What was he doing? Wasn't it too late to reconsider this marriage?

She squeezed his hand, hoping to jar him back to reality. His head immediately lifted. When his gaze met hers, she looked at him expectedly.

"I do." His response was faint.

The minister smiled and nodded. He turned to her. In a calm, steady voice, the minister said, "Do you, Carla Elana Falco, take Franco Giuseppe Marchello to be your husband?"

Her tongue stuck to the roof of her mouth. This was it. This was the final part. All she had to do was utter two little words. It'd seemed so simple when Franco had to do it. But now that it was her turn and all eyes were on her, she suddenly realized the enormity of saying *I do* and how it would have an enormous impact on her life—every single aspect of her life was about to change.

Franco squeezed her hand just as she had done for him. Her eyes rose to meet his. And in his intent gaze was the expectation that she would follow his lead and seal the deal. After all, this had been her idea in the first place.

She swallowed hard and couldn't help but wonder if this was going to be the biggest mistake of her life. And then she uttered in a strangled voice, "I do."

Relief reflected in Franco's dark eyes. Apparently he didn't want to be left standing at the altar. They turned to the minister, who said a few words and then declared them husband and wife.

"You may kiss the bride." The minister beamed at them.

Oh no! How could she have forgotten about this part? Because there was no way that they were going to seal this business deal with a kiss. That was simply above and beyond their agreement. Surely Franco would agree. After all, it wasn't like he was into her.

She turned to Franco to tell him that they could skip this part. Her gaze flickered to his. She could read the look in his eyes. It was one of desire. He was going to kiss her. Her pulse raced with anticipation. This shouldn't happen, but there was a part of her that had always wondered what it'd be like to be kissed by him.

His hands spanned her waist. As he drew her nearer, it was only natural for her to reach out to him, placing her hands on his broad shoulders to maintain her balance. Because there was no way she would voluntarily reach out to him— wanting to feel his powerful muscles beneath her fingertips.

And then, as though there was a magnetic

force drawing them together, she felt her body lean toward his. She felt helpless to resist the attraction. Her heart pitter-pattered faster, harder. It echoed in her ears.

As though time were suspended, everything moved in slow motion. Her husband was about to kiss her. She was married. *Married.* The word echoed in her mind.

In the next millisecond, she pressed against his hard, muscular chest. *Oh my!* The air stilled in her lungs. The initial protest evaporated.

The touch of his lips to hers settled her frantic thoughts, allowing her to focus on him and her—on this dizzying, delicious kiss. His touch was warm and firm. His lips moved slowly over hers. A moan swelled in her throat. No first kiss was supposed to be this good—this addictive.

She gave herself up to the moment. She leaned fully into his embrace, giving herself to him. Her lips began to move beneath his. Because she wasn't going to turn away from this most amazing experience. She never wanted this wondrous sensation to end—

Someone cleared their throat.

Carla was immediately jerked out of the trancelike state she'd been in. Her feet came crashing back down to earth. She jumped back. Heat rushed up her neck and set her cheeks aflame. Well, if she'd wanted to convince her father that this marriage was real, that should have done it.

She didn't dare look at her new husband. She didn't want him to see how his kiss had warmed her cheeks and shaken her to the core. Because none of this was real. The marriage wasn't real. This wedding wasn't real. And that kiss hadn't been real.

Sure, it had all happened, but it was all a show. She just couldn't get caught up in their playacting. And it was all her father's fault. If he wasn't such a stubborn man. If he wasn't willing to risk his life to keep working—keep making sure their company was ever expanding at an alarming pace—she wouldn't officially be Mrs. Franco Marchello. That acknowledgment made her heart leap into her throat.

Mrs. Franco Marchello. Oh my!

Wedding guests rushed forward to congratulate them, but she couldn't focus on anything but this insurmountable mistake she'd made. She went through the motions as her mind struggled with the reality of what they'd just done.

The one thing she knew was that there would be no more kissing Franco. No way. Because it was dangerous. She couldn't think straight when he was so close to her. And when his lips were touching hers, all she could think was how much she wanted more of him—so much more.

* * *

That had gone totally wrong.

He'd only meant to give her a brief, passive kiss.

Franco inwardly groaned as he realized the kiss had been anything but brief or passive. There had been sparks that he hadn't seen coming. Those sparks had ignited a flame. And now he couldn't get Carla out of his system.

And that shouldn't have happened. It was a total miscalculation on his part. Because Carla was the last person on the planet he should be kissing. It wasn't that he didn't find her attractive. He thought Carla was the most beautiful woman he'd ever known. Any man with an active pulse couldn't deny her beauty.

The problem was the fact that she was Carlo Falco's daughter. And he had been duly warned by his grandfather not to trust a Falco. That's why Franco had had his team of attorneys go over the marriage contract twice. It was ironclad. This knowledge still didn't help him breathe easier.

"You really outdid yourself." Carla smiled at him, as they stood off to the side of the party. She lowered her voice so as not to be overheard. "I thought it would just be a small, forgettable exchange of vows, but you made this whole experience a lot more enjoyable and less businesslike. Not that I've forgotten this is all business, but still it was nice. Thank you."

Her words shocked him—in a good way. He swallowed hard. "You're welcome. I'm glad you liked it."

"I did." And then she leaned in close. "I almost believed it was real."

"But it was real. And now we have a show to put on for our guests." As the music played in the background, he held his hand out to her. "Shall we, Mrs. Marchello?"

She placed her hand in his and they started toward the dance floor—

"Not so fast." Carlo Falco stepped in front of them. His face was full of color as his brows were drawn together in a formidable line. "We need to talk."

Franco gave Carla's hand a reassuring squeeze. "Let's step over there."

"Not you." Her father's deep voice rumbled with barely restrained anger.

Franco wasn't going to let Carla take the brunt of her father's anger alone. They'd agreed to this plan together, and they'd see it through together. "We're married now. If you have something to say about that, you can say it to both of us."

Carlo's gaze moved to his daughter. "Is that how it's going to be from now on? A Marchello is going to do all the talking for you?"

"Papa, calm down. There's no need to get so worked up."

Her father's gaze narrowed. "So does he speak for you?"

"No. I can speak for myself. But in this case, I agree with my husband—"

"Husband, ha! This sham of a marriage is never going to last. You only agreed to marry him to spite me. When you're ready to admit this was a mistake, you know where to find me."

"But Papa, wait—"

Carlo stormed off. His pace didn't so much as slow down as she continued to call out to him. Nor did he give her a backward glance. Franco supposed that was something else Carlo had in common with his grandfather—a short temper and the feeling that they knew what was best for those around them. It was a quite an assumption on their parts. Franco's muscles tensed with anger. Carla wiggled her fingers, letting him know he was squeezing her hand too tightly.

When he glanced at her, he noticed how her eyes shimmered with unshed tears. "It'll be okay." He wasn't certain of it, but those were the first comforting words that came to mind. "He just needs a little time to get used to the idea."

"I knew he'd be upset—" her voice wavered with emotion "—but I've never seen him that upset."

"You can't do anything about it now. Let it go

for the moment. You being miserable all evening won't change anything."

"But I should go talk to him."

"And tell him what? That you're going to cave in and dissolve our marriage? Remember why you did this."

She drew in an unsteady breath. "You're right. He needs to cool off. I'll reason with him tomorrow."

"It sounds like a plan." He sent her an encouraging smile. "Now, would you like to dance?"

It was then that she glanced around at all the people trying not to stare at them and failing miserably.

"I suppose we'd better." She didn't waste any time as she led him to the dance floor.

Once on the dance floor, she placed her hand in his. He pulled her close. As they moved around the temporary dance floor, his heart pounded. He told himself it was from the physical activity, but secretly he knew it was from holding his beautiful bride so close—so temptingly close.

Carla laid her head on his shoulder as the photographer took their photo. It was then that Franco smelled the peachy-floral scent of her hair. He inhaled deeper. Maybe this marriage thing wasn't going to be so bad after all.

Just then Carla's heel came down on his foot. He bit back a yelp of pain. He was suddenly jarred from his fantasy. He couldn't help but wonder if her misstep had been accidental or intentional. Because her movements had been smooth and graceful up until that point. Was it possible she'd read the direction of his thoughts?

With that in mind, he loosened his hold on her waist, allowing some more space between them. Maybe then he would cool down and his imagination wouldn't keep tiptoeing into forbidden territory.

CHAPTER SIX

FOR THE MOST PART, it had been an amazing evening.

She could have danced all night long.

With Franco's attentive assistance, Carla was finally able to shove the scene with her father to the back of her mind. She found herself smiling. Why not? The worst was over. They were married now. There was nothing to contemplate. The deed had been done.

Still, it was hard not to be utterly and totally distracted by her dashing husband. *Husband*. That was going to take some getting used to.

She had to admit that Franco and his assistant had planned a pretty awesome party. And she noticed him smiling throughout the evening filled with delicious food and endless dancing. Though he entertained the guests, he was still an attentive husband. What happened after this evening, well, she wasn't going to let her mind go there. At least not yet.

Franco stepped up to her. He held out a flute

of champagne. It wasn't her first or second glass that evening. At first, she'd been hesitant to drink any, but as the festive mood of the evening swept over her, she found herself letting her guard down and enjoying the evening. After all, she couldn't spend the next six months at odds with her husband.

But the evening was winding down, and guests were departing. And secretly she didn't want to see it end. She wasn't ready to go back to reality with its endless meetings and arduous negotiations.

"Did you enjoy yourself?" Franco asked.

"I had a delightful time." She sipped the sweet, bubbly champagne.

He arched a brow. "Truthfully?"

She took her finger and made an X over her chest. "Cross my heart."

Gianna approached them. She leaned forward and gave Carla a hug. "I'm so happy for you. And best of all, we're sisters-in-law. Isn't that awesome?"

Carla hadn't thought of that before. "Yes, it is."

She glanced over as the two brothers shook hands and then clapped each other on the back. Franco looked more relaxed now than she'd ever seen him. Maybe it was just the relief of this day being over. If so, she had to agree with him. It had been surprisingly fun, but now she was exhausted.

After a glowing Gianna and her clearly besotted husband left, Carla turned and was surprised to find some people still on the dance floor.

Franco held his hand out to her. "May I have this dance?"

"Haven't you had enough dancing?"

He smiled. "Not with my beautiful bride."

Heat rushed to her cheeks. Even though she knew he was still playing a part, she couldn't help getting caught up in the moment. And it was impossible for her to deny the way his words made her heart pitter-patter, even if she only admitted it to herself.

What would it hurt to let the charade continue just a little longer? After all, it was too late now to visit her father. And it was too late to do any business. So for the moment, she was all Franco's—so to speak.

Carla finished her glass of sparkling blue champagne. Her favorite. Then she placed her hand in his and they made their way to the dance floor. A slow ballad started to play as Franco pulled her into his arms. She didn't hesitate as he drew her in close. She told herself it was the effect of the bubbly that had her giving up on keeping a modest distance between them.

The softness of her curves pressed up against the hard planes of his muscled chest. The breath caught in her lungs as every nerve ending in her body tingled with desire. She closed her eyes and rested her head against his shoulder. After all, he was now legally her husband—why not enjoy the advantages of the situation?

They danced one slow song after the next. With her head turned in toward his neck, she inhaled the scent of soap combined with a spiciness. It was utterly addictive and totally intoxicating. She was even tempted to press her lips to his neck. She wondered how he'd react. She should do it. She'd thrown all other caution to the wind today.

At the last moment, she restrained her impish impulses. That would be taking their charade too far, right? She couldn't possibly have Franco brush off her advances. If so, how would she ever live with him for the next six months? Therefore, she had to tamp down these unexpected and unwanted desires. But that was easier said than done, because her body refused to abide. Instead of stepping back and allowing space between them, she stayed right there pressed up against him.

All the while their bodies brushed together and an undeniable flame of desire was building into a massive inferno that threatened to consume her. What was Franco thinking? Did he desire her as much as she wanted him?

She thought of lifting her head to look into

his eyes and ask him, but she didn't have the nerve to do it. Because while she was looking for signs of desire in his eyes, he'd be able to see her own growing desire for him. It was best to stay where she was. Because when he held her so close, there was no way he could read anything in her expression. As for body language, well, that was a totally different subject.

Franco stopped moving. Disappointment swelled up within her. With great regret, she lifted her head. "You don't want to dance any longer?"

He smiled at her. "The music has stopped, *amore*."

She tried to listen over the pounding of her heart. It was then that she realized the music had indeed stopped. And when she glanced around, she found they were alone on the dance floor.

"Where did everyone go?"

"Home, I imagine."

The only others were the band and some servers who were clearing the last of the glasses. A sense of disappointment came over her when she realized the celebration was over. She understood the absurdity of such a thought, because in the beginning she'd been the one dreading this wedding. And yet Franco had gone out of his way to make it a very enjoyable evening.

As a cool breeze off the lake brushed over her bare skin, she found herself rubbing her arms.

With autumn not far off, the evenings were growing much cooler. Funny that she hadn't noticed the dip in the temperature at all when she'd been wrapped in Franco's arms.

"Shall we go inside?" Franco asked.

"We're staying here tonight?"

"Yes. Is that a problem?"

She thought about it for a moment. It wasn't like she had anyone waiting for her at home. She had her own apartment and didn't so much as have a pet. So there was no one to miss her. And she'd already made arrangements with her father's live-in companion to keep an extra close eye on Carlo this evening.

"It's no problem at all. Tomorrow will be soon enough to adjust to the reality of our new situation."

He once more offered his arm to her. Who would have thought that Franco Marchello was such a gentleman? She smiled as she slipped her hand into the crook of his arm. They strolled into the villa that had obviously just been renovated. Everything inside was shiny and new.

They kicked off their shoes by the door. It was only then that Carla realized how sore her feet were from dancing in heels all evening. But she'd been so caught up in the festivities that she hadn't noticed until now.

Franco slipped off his tux jacket. He removed the black tie and then he unbuttoned the collar.

He undid his cuff links and rolled up his sleeves. Though it was a much more casual look, it made him look even more attractive—like a real-life James Bond.

While Franco set to work building a fire in the living room's stone fireplace, she poured them some more bubbly. In her nervousness, she filled the glasses a bit too much. Oh well, it was a night for celebrating. She held out a glass to him.

When Franco resisted taking the glass, she said, "Go ahead. We have a lot to celebrate."

"We do?"

She nodded. "Our plan is underway. Tomorrow you and I will start figuring out the best way to advance both of our companies. I see a beautiful future for both of us."

He clinked his glass against hers. "I'm looking forward to it. But business will come soon enough. Let's just focus on the here and now." They settled on the couch and sipped the sparkling wine. "Did you enjoy the day?"

"Other than the scene with my father, it was a wonderful wedding."

His gaze flickered to hers and then moved back to the fire. "If you're having regrets, it's not too late to back out."

She shook her head. The truth was she'd never considered getting married against her father's wishes. "If this had been a real wedding, yes, it would have been unbearable. It's hard enough not having my mother in my life. I miss her every day—every time I need some advice. With my father being my only living parent, I just can't imagine having him angry at me if this were a real wedding, but luckily it's not." Then realizing how that might sound, she said, "You know what I mean."

Franco nodded. "He loves you a lot. That much is very obvious."

"I don't know if he loves me a lot. People that love you don't normally push you into a marriage you don't want or block you from taking over the business when it's for their own welfare. And then get furious when you finally marry like they wanted."

"That's not exactly fair. You know how he feels about my family. You knew he wouldn't take it well."

"I just wish he trusted me to know what's right for me and would stop trying to push me into what he thinks I should do."

"I think he's done all of it because he's worried something might happen to him and he doesn't want you to end up alone."

It wasn't like she was a child. She could pick out her own husband—just like she'd done. Not that Franco was really her husband—well, legally he was, but not in her heart.

She decided it was best to skip over the marriage and husband part; instead she asked, "Then why doesn't he trust me with what he loves most in this world—the restaurants?"

Franco paused as though giving her question due consideration. Then he rubbed the back of his neck. "I wish I could give you an answer, but I have no idea. You're very smart, well-educated and full of energy. I think he's foolish for wanting someone else to fill in for him."

His spontaneous compliments warmed a spot in her chest. "You really think I'm that well suited for the position?"

His gaze once more met hers. "I do. You'd be my first pick."

"Thank you." She smiled at him. She had no idea that he thought so highly of her. It was like he'd bestowed yet another wedding gift upon her—one that meant so much more than the designer wedding dress or the glittering diamond wedding band.

Her gaze lowered and she lifted her hand ever so slightly, letting the firelight play over the arrangement of diamonds encompassing her finger. He certainly hadn't withheld anything for this marriage—even if it was only a temporary one.

She wondered what his extravagance meant. Did he wish there was more to this marriage than there was? Her heart fluttered at the thought. Or was this just his generous way?

It was at this point that she realized just how much she didn't know about her extremely handsome and mysterious husband. And since they'd already talked about her complicated relationship with her father, it was time she learned a bit more about the man she was married to.

"And what about you?" she asked. "What was it like to get married without not only your grandparents but your mother and father as well?"

He sighed and leaned his head back against the couch. As he moved, he slid a little closer to her, making her heart pitter-pat faster. "If this was a real wedding, I couldn't have done it without inviting my grandparents. For better or worse, they've always been there for me—even when my grandfather vehemently disagreed with me."

"I'm glad you have them. But what about your parents? I've noticed you never mention them."

"What's to mention? My father is like some distant uncle that stops by once in a blue moon when he's in town and is gone again before any meaningful connection can be established. And my mother, well, she's around for the important events, but her focus is always on her ever-revolving romances."

"I'm sorry." Carla didn't know what else to say.

Her mother had always been there for her—

right up until she died. Even hiding the truth of her illness from her so she wouldn't have to worry. Though Carla would have much rather known about the severity of her mother's illness. She might have done things differently. Might have stopped what she was doing to spend those last days with her mother. But this conversation wasn't about her.

"It's okay." The anguished tone of his voice said it was anything but okay.

Her heart ached for that little boy who'd been tossed aside and forgotten. How could someone do that to their child? It was unimaginable.

She swallowed her rising emotions. "That must have been so hard for a young boy not to have either of his parents around."

"I figure they had their reasons to keep their distance. After all, my grandfather isn't an easy man to deal with."

"You think that's the reason they left."

He shrugged. "I think it's my father's reason, but not my mother's. She doesn't listen to anyone but herself. But my father, well, I think he couldn't do anything right in my grandfather's eyes, and he got tired of trying."

"But why would they leave you and your brother?"

"I'm not sure. I wouldn't put it past my grandfather to threaten to fight for custody of us. After all, we are the heirs to the Marchello estate. And without my father around, we were even more important to him."

Sympathy welled up in her for the little boy Franco had once been, who didn't understand why both of his parents had disappeared from his life. How could his parents just abandon him and his brother? Who did such a thing?

She turned to Franco to tell him how sorry she felt for him, but when his gaze met hers, she immediately forgot what she'd been about to say. The longer they gazed into each other's eyes, the faster her heart beat.

Had he moved closer to her? Because their shoulders were now touching. Or was it possible that she had leaned over toward him? There was this undeniable desire drawing them together. Her entire body tingled with an excited awareness.

When it came to husbands, she'd definitely come up with a winning one. There was no denying that he was handsome, but even more than that he was thoughtful. What kind of man went to all this trouble for a wife in name only?

She couldn't even fathom the extremes he would go to for a woman he loved. And she didn't want to imagine it. Not now. Not in this moment.

Because no matter their reason for exchanging wedding vows, the truth of the matter was that they were legally husband and wife. And though she wanted to tell herself that it was all a business arrangement, she couldn't deny that there had been a definite shift in the ground beneath her feet when she'd said *I do.*

And now when she stared at her newly minted husband, she wondered if that kiss they'd shared when the minister had pronounced them husband and wife had been real. Because she'd swear her feet had been floating above the ground. It was that good—that heart-poundingly amazing.

A loud pop of wood in the fireplace made her jump. The champagne sloshed over the sides of her glass and dripped down over her fingers. When she glanced down at the sticky mess, she realized that it had spilled onto Franco's white dress shirt.

"Oh no. I'm so sorry."

"No big deal."

She was horrified. "I'll get something to dry it." She spotted some napkins placed next to trays of finger foods left for them by the catering staff. She grabbed a napkin and then turned to Franco.

As she knelt on the couch next to him, she pressed the napkin to his abdomen. Being left-handed, she had no choice but to place her other hand on his chest to keep herself from falling into him.

She ran the white cloth up his side, all the

while feeling the steely strength of his muscles. Her mouth grew dry. She didn't dare meet his gaze. He'd know where her thoughts had strayed.

"If you were trying to cool things off between us," he said in a deep, gravelly voice, "it isn't working." And then he moved to unbutton his shirt.

Carla's mouth grew dry as she watched him undo one button and then the next. "What... what are you doing?"

A little smile lifted the corners of his mouth. "Taking off my wet shirt so you won't worry about it any longer."

She sat back on her heels as he pulled his shirt free. She shouldn't be sitting there openly staring at him, but she was helpless to stop. His chest was so toned, it was though he spent every day at the gym. His tanned skin was smooth, and his chest had a smattering of dark curls. Wow!

Her fingers tingled to reach out and work their way up his torso. She resisted the urge. She wasn't quite sure how that was possible. Maybe it was the fact that at this moment her mind was overwhelmed with everything that had happened today.

She finally dragged her gaze up to meet his. She didn't know what she expected to find, but it sure wasn't the desire flickering in his eyes, mirroring her own rising needs.

One moment, she was sitting there looking at him, and in the next his lips were pressing to hers. If she thought their first kiss as husband and wife had been something, it was nothing compared to this passionate embrace.

Without an audience, there was no need to hold back. And he most certainly didn't as he wrapped his arms around her, deepening the kiss. Then, using those muscles she'd been admiring, he swept her into his arms and repositioned them so she was lying back on the couch. He settled on top of her—the full, lean length of him. And they were still kissing—oh, were they kissing.

And right now, Carla had absolutely no desire to stop this delicious moment. After all, what was to stop them? For the next six months, he was her husband. And yes, maybe they had made some initial ground rules about what was expected from the marriage, but as his mouth moved over hers and her fingers trailed over his bare shoulders, she couldn't quite recall what those ground rules had been.

CHAPTER SEVEN

LAST NIGHT HAD been a mistake.

A complete and total mistake.

Franco couldn't believe he'd let himself spend the entire night with his new bride. It had been the most amazing evening—one he wasn't soon to forget. Oh, who was he kidding? He was never going to forget it. Carla was the type of woman who left her mark upon your life.

He raked his fingers through his hair as he paced back and forth in the living room. He hadn't even been married for twenty-four hours before he'd broken their agreement to keep things uncomplicated and totally platonic.

Luckily for him, Carla had still been asleep when he'd awoken that morning. But he knew she'd be up soon, and then what would he say to her? How would he explain how he'd let things get totally and absolutely out of control?

As his mind rolled back over the highlights of their evening together, a smile pulled at the corners of his mouth. So maybe it wasn't all bad. In fact, it had been quite good—

"Morning."

At the sound of Carla's voice, the smile slipped from his face. Hesitantly, he turned. Carla wasn't smiling but she wasn't frowning, either. His body tensed as he waited for her to start yelling at him about how he'd broken all the rules when he'd slipped off his shirt and then proceeded to kiss her.

He could blame it on the alcohol, but that wasn't the truth. The fact was he'd been fantasizing about kissing again her ever since they'd been pronounced—he hesitated, still not at all comfortable with their new marital status— since they'd formalized their agreement. It was in that moment—with the memory of them taking a vow of forever, in sickness and in health— that he came back to reality. The excitement of the evening wore off and he could finally think straight once more.

He cleared his throat. "Morning. There's coffee in the kitchen."

"Thank you." When she smiled, he felt his heart beat faster.

He struggled not to return the smile. It was better to cool things off now before either of them got in too deep and ended up getting hurt in the end. And there would be an end. He didn't believe in marriage—in forever. And this was just a business arrangement, nothing more.

When Carla turned toward the kitchen, he followed her. "I was thinking we should get back to the city as soon as you're ready."

She poured herself a cup of coffee. "I'm sorry I slept so late." She yawned. "I'm just really tired."

Her back was to him, so he wasn't able to read the look on her face. He shifted his weight from one foot to the other. "About last night— it was a mistake."

Carla spun around. Her gaze narrowed on him. For a moment, she didn't say anything. This just made him all the more uncomfortable. He couldn't help but wonder if that had been her intent.

Still, the longer the silence lingered, the more awkward the moment became. So he said, "I don't want to hurt you. And if I let you think this is the beginning of something, it'd be a lie—"

"Good. I was hoping you didn't get the wrong idea, either." Her voice was calm and restrained.

It wasn't the reaction he'd been anticipating. Most women he'd been involved with always wanted more than he could offer. And some got very angry when he set them straight.

She took a big gulp of coffee before turning to him. "I just have to run upstairs and grab my stuff. Then we can go." When her dismissal of their lovemaking left him speechless, she asked, "Is there something else?"

"Um, no. So we're all right?"

"Sure." Her voice was light and upbeat. "Why wouldn't we be?"

And with that she sailed out of the kitchen with her coffee cup in hand. He was left standing there with his mouth hanging open. Had that just happened? Was his lovemaking that unremarkable?

Disappointment assailed him. He didn't know what he'd been expecting from her, but it hadn't been a complete dismissal of their passionate night. He should be happy. This gave them a chance for a do-over—a chance to keep things purely platonic.

But he knew any attempt to forget what they'd shared the night before was going to be difficult. No. It was going to be a downright impossible feat. There was no forgetting Carla.

She had to get away.

Her bare feet moved up the steps silently.

Carla tripped at the top of staircase in her haste to get away from Franco. Her free hand reached out, grabbing the banister. Luckily she'd drunk enough of the coffee that it hadn't splashed over the side.

She didn't tarry on the landing. The last thing she wanted was to face Franco again so soon.

She didn't want him to know how his words in the kitchen had cut her deeply. And she had a sinking feeling that her disappointment and pain were written all over her face. How she'd kept it all together in front of him had been her best acting job ever.

She rushed inside the bedroom she'd shared with Franco. With the door shut, she leaned back against it. Her vision blurred. Tears threatened to spill onto her cheeks.

She grew angry with herself for getting worked up. But when he'd so easily dismissed their lovemaking—a night that felt like it was the beginning of something real between them—she'd felt as though she'd been cut to the quick. She didn't readily open herself to someone like she had with Franco.

Maybe it was the wedding vows—to love, honor and cherish. Or maybe it was the litany of romantic ballads they'd danced to all evening. Or maybe it was a bit too much champagne. Or perhaps it was a lethal combination of all those things that had had her letting down her guard last night. Franco had gotten closer to her than any other man had ever done, including her loser ex-fiancé.

And worse yet was she'd let herself fall into a false sense of security with Franco's soul-stirring kisses, his gentle caresses and his endearing words. Ugh! What was wrong with her? He was probably that way with all his women—

She halted her thoughts right there. She just couldn't deal with the thought of him being so loving and attentive with anyone else. Maybe it had been a one-night sort of thing, but she wanted to believe that it was special. She wanted to think their night together had been unique for both of them. Even if it wasn't going to happen ever again.

Because whether she liked it or not, Franco was right. They'd agreed not to let things get messy for a reason. It was best not to get caught up in some fantasy, because in the end she'd get hurt. Because Franco didn't do relationships, unless they were of the business variety.

They only had six months in which to make their plan a reality. And if they were so wrapped up in—well, whatever happened last night— they wouldn't put all their energy into making this venture a huge success.

She quickly grabbed her things—including her wedding dress—and headed for the door. It was time they got back to reality. She was certain once she was home that they would be able to keep the lines in their relationship straight. There would be no more confusion—no more kisses or anything else.

CHAPTER EIGHT

THE RIDE BACK to Verona seemed to go on forever.

Carla couldn't wait to step in her apartment. She just wanted a few minutes to herself before she faced her father. Being back among her things would make her feel grounded—make her feel more like herself—not like Mrs. Marchello.

But when they reached the city, Franco didn't make the turn toward her place. "Wait. You missed the turn."

"No, I didn't."

Of course he did. "My place is the other way."

"And my place is this way."

"But I don't want to go to your place. I have to go see my father."

As Franco maneuvered the car along the sparsely filled road, he chanced a quick glance at her. "You do realize that you're going to have to move into my place, don't you?"

"What? No. No. That isn't going to happen." She crossed her arms.

In a gentle, nonaggressive voice, he said, "Don't you think it's going to look strange to people if we live apart?"

She inwardly groaned. Why did everything that had to do with Franco have to be so complicated? Maybe in her haste to figure out all the legal ramifications and rushing to make sure her father was sufficiently looked after, she might have missed some of the complications of this plan.

She wanted to argue with Franco. She wanted to tell him that it would be totally fine if they lived separately, but she knew that none of that was true. Drat him for being so logical.

"Fine," she said, "You can move into my place."

"I don't think so."

She turned to him. "Why not? It has two bedrooms."

"I've been to your place to drop off papers, and I've seen how small it is compared to my penthouse. Trust me. We'll be much more comfortable at my place."

Trust him? The echo of her father's warning rang in her ears. She'd trusted Franco last night by letting him see a vulnerable side of her, and look where that had gotten her. He'd brushed her off in the light of day, leaving her pride sporting a painful bruise.

She'd trusted her ex and he'd cheated on her, all the while boldly lying to her face about the reason for delaying their wedding. And then there was her father, who'd taught her that trust was supposed to go both ways. And yet he staunchly refused to trust that she was making the right choices for the right reasons.

So no, she wasn't ready to trust Franco so easily. And she wasn't ready to give in on their living arrangements just because he said so. "But my place is closer to the office."

"Your office. Not mine. My place is between them both."

That much was true. She was running out of reasons why they should stay at her place instead of his. And quite honestly, she just didn't have the gumption to keep fighting him over this. As it was, she had to deal with her father in the near future. She was going to need all her energy to deal with him and make sure her marriage to Franco didn't cause him to have a medical setback.

"Okay," she said softly.

"Excuse me, did you just agree to stay at my place?"

"Yes! Yes, I did. But don't push it."

He was quiet for a moment as he negotiated a

busy intersection. "Do you want to move your things now?"

"No. I need to go to my place, change clothes and go see my father. It's time he knows that I intend to take over control of the company. Immediately."

"Agreed. I'll go with you."

"Absolutely not!"

Franco slowed the car as he pulled off into a parking spot. "Why not? I'm your husband."

She shook her head. "It'll be too much for him with you there."

"What do you mean, too much?"

There was quite a bit she'd failed to tell Franco about the true reason behind her move to take over the company. Because when all was said and done, she was willing to give up the company. However, she wasn't ready to lose her father.

"Just trust me." She pleaded with him with her eyes, hoping he'd let the subject rest.

The truth of the matter was that she hadn't wanted to dig into the painful details. She would do whatever it took to see that her father was well taken care of since that stubborn man wouldn't do it himself. And no, she didn't want Franco to see her vulnerable again.

Franco's dark gaze probed her. "If we're going to trust each other, we have to start talking to each other."

He was right. Maybe if they'd slowed down long enough to talk last night, they'd have reminded each other of the rules of their marriage, but instead they'd let their desires take over and everything had spiraled out of control. It was a lesson learned.

She glanced down at her clasped hands in her lap. Memories flashed in her mind of seeing her father in a hospital bed. Not once. But twice. She wrung her hands together.

And the last time he was in the hospital, with all the wires connected to his chest and the IV in his arm, his complexion had been the same pale shade as his white sheets. Her tattered heart had tumbled down to her heels.

Carla closed her eyes, willing away the troubling images. She couldn't go through that again. She couldn't lose him already. Because if she did—if she lost him—she'd be all alone in this world. And she wasn't ready for that, either.

Sure, there was Gianna, but she was happily married now and expecting her first baby. She wouldn't have the time to spend with Carla like they'd done in the past. And though she was immensely happy for her cousin, she knew that things would never be the same again.

But how did she explain any of this to Franco without him seeing her as weak? Because when it came down to it, they were now business partners. And there would be a lot of negotiating in the future of how to handle this venture between her national restaurant chain and his expansive line of spices. It would be quite an endeavor—one where she needed to hold a strong edge so as not to be bulldozed by him and his narrowed pursuits.

"It's my father." She hesitated, trying to tamp down her rising emotions.

"I know he isn't happy about our marriage, but there's no way he can break the contract as long as we're married. My attorneys went over everything. They said it was as ironclad as they'd ever seen."

She shook her head. "It's not about the contract."

"Then what is it?" His voice was soft and coaxing.

What would it hurt to tell him? Sure, she'd promised her father not to disclose information about his second heart attack because he'd been worried that his business associates would view him as weak. Her father was the strongest, proudest man she'd ever known.

And telling Franco now when her father was out of the hospital and doing well, according to his physicians, wouldn't be a big deal. After all, Franco was now her husband. And maybe if he understood why their combined effort to put his spices in her restaurants was so important to her, he'd be more of an ally than an advisory. Secretly she longed for Franco to be on her side. Otherwise these next six months were going to drag on forever.

"You know that my father had a heart attack the night of Gianna's wedding, but what you don't know is that just recently he'd had a second heart attack, and this time they had to do bypass surgery."

Sympathy reflected in Franco's eyes. "I'm so sorry."

"He doesn't want anyone to know."

"Why not?"

"He's afraid people in the business world will treat him differently. But while he's worried about getting back to work, the doctors are worried that with the amount of damage to his heart, running a business of that size will be too much for him." Her voice wobbled with emotion. "And I just can't lose him. Not yet."

Franco reached out and pulled her close so her head rested on his shoulder. "He'll be all right."

She wanted to believe him. "So you see why you can't come with me today. I just can't risk getting him too upset."

"I understand."

One man in her life understood her decisions, but would the other one be as understanding? She had her doubts.

* * *

Everything was changing so quickly.

Carla hadn't lingered at her place. She'd quickly packed the essentials and then headed to her father's house. She told herself that she was in a rush to get back to work—not to see her husband again, even if he was so easy on the eyes.

But first, she had to speak with her father. She found him in his home office. "Hello, Papa."

He glanced up from the paper he was reading. He slid off his reading glasses. "What are you doing here?"

"Hello to you, too." She sensed his bad mood hadn't faded like she'd hoped. She nervously spun her wedding rings around her finger. "What have you been up to?"

He sat forward, resting his arms on the desk. "The real question is why have you married a Marchello?"

The sight of his pale complexion and gaunt cheeks had tears stinging the backs of Carla's eyes and silenced the rebuttal in the back of her throat. Not so long ago, he'd been the strongest man she'd ever known. But not one but two heart attacks had taken their toll on him. He was different now. He constantly hovered over her as though he didn't trust her judgment where business was concerned or even her personal life. She'd endured it because she didn't want to do anything to get him worked up. But things couldn't continue that way.

"Tell me you came to your senses and backed out of that marriage." Her father's voice was still deep and vibrant. His sharp gaze needled her.

She swallowed hard. "No. Franco is a good guy." She truly believed that or she wouldn't have gone through with this plan. "You just need to give him a chance."

Her father shook his head in disapproval. "Don't trust him. The Marchellos cannot be trusted."

"Why?"

Her father grunted. "The details don't matter. Just heed my warning."

"This grudge or whatever it is, is it the reason you no longer carry their products in our restaurants?"

"It is. Trust me, it's for the best." And then he quirked a brow at her. "How did you know?" Before she could answer, he said, "You've been talking to Franco."

"I have. He's my husband."

"You can tell him that as long as I live, his family's products won't be in any of our establishments. Ever."

"Even if it's good business?"

"Doing business with a Marchello is never good business."

"I won't waste my time trying to convince

you otherwise. Just know now that I'm married, I'll be assuming full control of the company while you recuperate. And you might as well know that I'll be reintroducing the Marchello Spices in the restaurants."

Her father's bushy brows rose. "You can't do that!"

"But I can. Remember the deal we signed?"

He pointed at her. "You tricked me."

"No, I didn't. I simply did what you wanted—I got married."

"You were supposed to marry a good and honest man." His hands waved through the air as he talked.

"I did. If you would just give him a chance—"

"I won't. I refuse." He crossed his arms over his chest.

She wasn't going to push the subject. "Have you been monitoring your blood pressure and writing it down like they told you at the hospital?"

"Yes."

"And taking all your meds?"

"I can take care of myself. Now go."

"But Papa—"

"I said go." His voice boomed in the office.

She didn't want to leave him like this, but she didn't see where she had much of a choice. With her being there, he was just getting more worked up. And it wasn't like he lived alone.

Since his first heart attack, she'd hired him a live-in companion.

She turned and headed for the door. She hesitated in the doorway and then turned back. "I'm happy. I just thought you'd want to know."

Her father's gaze met hers, but he didn't say anything.

She walked off to find Aldo and let him know that her father was still agitated, so he should keep a close eye on him that evening. She'd gotten married and assumed control of the company with her father's best interest in mind. He'd see that when he calmed down. She hoped.

CHAPTER NINE

CARLA HAD GONE directly from her father's house to the office. Still upset with both of the men in her life, she immersed herself in her work. Thankfully there was a lot of it.

Not in the mood to speak to anyone, she silenced her phone and let the calls go to voice mail. Of course, she kept an eye on the caller ID just in case it was anything about her father.

There was one call from Gianna. Two from business associates and an amazing four calls from her—erm, from Franco. But considering how easily he'd dismissed their night of lovemaking, she didn't feel compelled to stop what she was doing to take his call.

Even though she'd only been out of the office a day and a half, her email was overflowing. By the time she'd sorted through them, it was past dinnertime.

Part of her felt guilty for not telling Franco that she wouldn't be around for dinner, but the other part said they were roommates at best and she didn't owe him updates on her schedule. The truth was that she had no idea how to act toward her husband who wasn't really her husband. It was so confusing.

When she arrived at the penthouse, it was getting late. She felt weird about being there. She let herself inside with the key Franco had given her. This was only her second time there. The first time had been to go over some items in the marriage contract.

"Franco?" She paused inside the door with two bags slung over each shoulder and a big suitcase with wheels.

The lighting in the apartment was dim. And she didn't hear anything. Was he even home? She recalled his phone calls. Maybe she should have answered. Did he leave her a voice mail? She fumbled with her purse to retrieve her phone—

"Carla, you're here." Franco stepped into the spacious foyer. He looked relaxed, with his hair a bit scattered, the top buttons on his shirt undone, and he was walking around in his bare feet. "I wasn't sure what time you'd be home. I tried to call you."

"Sorry I missed your call. I was buried in work." Heat warmed her cheeks. "You know how it is when you've been out of the office for a while."

"Here." He stepped up to her. "Let me take

those for you." When she relinquished her load, he said, "I'll put these in your room."

"Thank you."

"You can make yourself comfortable in the living room. I just had a pizza delivered. Help yourself to it." And then he set off with her luggage.

Guilt assailed her. Here he was being all nice and thoughtful while she'd been ducking his calls. She placed her purse and phone on the large square coffee table where she noticed Franco's phone and a fat manila folder. It appeared he'd been working at home.

Remembering her way to the guest bathroom, she freshened up. When she returned to the living room, she found Franco sitting there. He served up a slice of pizza for each of them. For a moment they ate in silence. With her stomach knotted up most of the day, she hadn't eaten much. As she kicked off her heels and curled up on the large couch, she found her hunger had returned. She devoured her slice of pizza.

Carla served them each another slice. "I'm really sorry about turning off my ringer."

"It's okay. I've been known to do that a time or two." He sent her a reassuring smile. "How did things go with your father?"

She found herself opening up about the whole awful affair. It all came tumbling out, and it felt good to get it out there.

Sympathy reflected in Franco's eyes. "I'm really sorry—"

"You have nothing to be sorry about. This whole marriage thing was my idea. I knew it wouldn't go over well, but I didn't think he'd be this mad."

"Do you want me to speak to him?"

"No." She shook her head. "Thank you, but I think that would just make everything worse."

"I'm sure he'll come around. Just give him a little time."

She nodded. "I'm sure you're right."

While they finished the rest of their pizza in silence, Franco turned on the television to a police drama. She got drawn into it, but her eyelids grew heavy. She leaned back on the couch. She just needed to close her eyes for a moment. Just a moment.

"Carla?"

She heard her name being called, but she wasn't ready to move. She was so warm and comfortable. And she'd been dreaming that she was wrapped in Franco's arms as he led her around the dance floor. She didn't want it to end, because by the look in his eyes, she was certain he was about to kiss her—

"Carla?" Someone jostled her.

Still in a sleepy fog, she leaned forward, pressing her lips to his. His touch was warm and gentle. Her lips moved over his. Her fingers reached out, stroking the stubble on his cheek. In her mind they were standing in the middle of a grand dance floor with white glitter lights all around them. She was wearing a flowing white wedding dress, and Franco looked dashing in his black tux. And she pulled back to tell him that she loved him. He spoke her name. Was he going to say *I love you* first?

"Carla? Carla, wake up."

Her eyes flew open. It took her a moment to gain her bearings. And then with horror, she realized she'd dozed off with her head on Franco's shoulder.

She sat straight up. "I'm sorry. I must have been more tired than I thought." Heat warmed her face as she fumbled to grab her phone and purse. "I should go to bed."

"Do you want me to show you to your room?"

She shook her head, still not looking at him. "I've got it. Um…good night."

And then she set off in the direction she'd seen Franco take her luggage. The bedroom was done up in tans and blues. A big sleigh bed dominated the room, but there was no sign of her luggage.

She moved to the other side of the hallway. This bedroom was done up in peaches and cream. When she spotted her luggage, she knew she was in the right place. She stepped inside the room and closed the door.

She pressed her back against the door and closed her eyes. What must Franco think of her? How had she ended up draped against him? Just the thought brought the heat back to her face. At least she hadn't talked in her sleep—had she?

With a groan, she moved away from the door. She glanced around the modern bedroom with its minimalist decor. She tried to decide if this was Franco's taste in decorating or if he just hadn't bothered to take the time or effort to add some personality to the apartment. She shrugged and turned to the bags Franco had insisted on carrying for her. They were now spread out over the king-size four-poster bed.

She pushed the memory of that vivid dream to the back of her mind. Even before it, she hadn't been sure how to act around him. Maybe they just had to figure out this new development in their relationship. And they'd have plenty of time now that they were not only living in his penthouse but also working together.

The only thing she did know was that her father was wrong about Franco. Maybe his grandfather was a liar, but not Franco. If her father would just give him a chance, he would realize what a kind and upstanding guy he was—a man they could conduct a successful business deal with.

Carla set to work, unpacking her things and placing them in the empty walk-in closet. She decided to look upon this temporary move as an adventure. And in the end, they would all get what they wanted.

Most of her clothes were hung up when her phone rang. She rushed over to the bed. The caller ID displayed the name of her assistant, Rosa. It was strange for her to call her so late, but since Carla had been out of the office for the wedding, things had piled up. Maybe she'd missed something urgent when she'd been at the office earlier.

She immediately pressed the phone to her ear. "Rosa, what's wrong?"

"This isn't Rosa, it's Rose. And why are you answering my boyfriend's phone?" The high-pitched voice hit the wrong chord in Carla.

Was it possible she'd grabbed Franco's phone instead of her own? "Who's your boyfriend?"

"Franco Marchello. Now put him on the phone."

So it was true. She was holding Franco's phone. Her grip tightened. He'd told her that he wasn't seeing anyone. Had he lied to her?

In her mind, she heard her father saying, *"I told you so. You can't trust a Marchello."* Immediately anger pulsed through her veins. She refused to be made a fool of.

"Franco can't come to the phone." Carla wasn't sure how she kept her voice so calm and level, because she was anything but that on the inside.

"Who is this? Is this his assistant?"

"No. This is his wife. And I'd appreciate it if you wouldn't call my husband again." And then she disconnected the call.

She rushed out of her room, hoping to find Franco in the living room. He wasn't there. She checked the kitchen, but the lights were out. She turned to look at the door just off the kitchen—Franco's bedroom door.

She was pretty certain if he'd gone out that he would have let her know. That meant he must be in there. It was the last place she wanted to speak with him, but this wasn't going to wait. She needed her phone back.

She marched to the other side of the apartment and rapped her knuckles on the door.

"Hang on," he called out.

She didn't want to wait. She didn't want to see him. How dare he make a fool of her? With each passing second, her temper rose. She seesawed between telling him exactly what she thought of him and keeping her emotions to herself, not letting him see that it got to her.

When the door swung open, Franco stood there shirtless, showing off his muscular chest with broad shoulders. A pair of navy boxers hugged his trim waist. "Hi. Did you need something? More towels?"

"Uh...no." She struggled to drag her gaze back to his face.

He smiled as amusement twinkled in his eyes. He propped himself against the door. "I'm not a mind reader, so you'll have to tell me what has brought you to my door." And then his eyes widened as though he'd figured out what she wanted—him. He opened the door wider. "You can come in."

Heat swirled in her chest and rushed to her cheeks. How dare he think she was going to sleep with him again? If he thought he could have her and a girlfriend on the side, he was very wrong.

"I trusted you to keep your word," she said, trying to keep her emotions at bay. "I knew going into this arrangement that it would be hard—it would definitely have its challenges. But I thought you and I were adult enough to handle it."

He raked his fingers through his hair, scattering the short dark strands. "What are you talking about?"

She glared at him. He was playing with her and seeing what she knew. What if there was more that she didn't know—more women she didn't know about? An uneasy feeling churned in the pit of her stomach. She refused to acknowledge that the feeling eating at her felt a lot like jealousy. She was not jealous. Not. At. All.

She refused to play into his game. "Like you don't know what you've been up to and with whom."

"I don't or I wouldn't have asked you."

"Either adhere to our legal agreement or I'll sue you for breach of contract." She held out his phone. "Our phones got mixed up. I'd like mine back."

His eyes widened as his lips formed an O. He retreated to the table next to his great big bed, and she couldn't help but wonder how many times Rose had been in this room. Carla immediately stopped the thought. She wasn't going there. What he did before their marriage was none of her business. He just had to follow their agreement while he was her husband. It wasn't too much to expect.

He returned to the doorway where she'd remained. "Listen, I don't know what you think is going on, but I can assure you that there's been a misunderstanding."

Her unwavering gaze met his. "I didn't misunderstand anything. But you might want to have that conversation with your girlfriend."

She grabbed her phone from his hand and then returned his phone. Not waiting for him to say anything further, she turned and headed back across the hallway. It wasn't until she was inside her room with the door shut that she expelled a pent-up breath.

Did he really think she didn't know what he was up to? She wouldn't stand for him sneaking around behind her back. She told herself it was all about them adhering to the deal and it had absolutely nothing to do with not being able to stand the thought of Franco holding another woman in his arms and kissing her the way he'd kissed Carla. None at all.

What in the world had gotten her so worked up?

And why did she suddenly think he had a girlfriend? A wife was plenty for him. There was no way he'd want to please two women at once. That would be a very dangerous proposition. He shook his head, chasing away the troubling images.

But if Carla was truly his wife in every sense of the word, did she really think another woman could tempt him away? Definitely not.

It didn't take Franco long to realize that a woman he'd briefly seen before he'd met Carla had phoned. He inwardly groaned. The woman was trouble. The last he knew, she'd been called away for a lengthy business arrangement in the United Arab Emirates.

He didn't want to call Rose. In fact, it was the very last thing he wanted to do, but with Carla having a total fit, he had to know what Rose had said to her so he could try and undo it. Because while he didn't care what Rose thought about him, he cared very much what Carla thought.

The conversation with Rose was mostly one-sided as she regaled him with all her business triumphs in the United Arab Emirates. Every time he interrupted her in order to cut to the chase, she started over and the conversation just went on and on.

Sometime around midnight, they finally got around to the part he'd been waiting for—Rose's conversation with Carla—the one where she'd introduced herself as his girlfriend. Franco had inwardly groaned. She wanted to know if it was true that he was now married. He'd told her he was and happily so. Rose was furious. She accused him of leading her on and that she would never forgive him. She hung up on him, which was fine by him. And then he blocked her number, which was something he should have done long ago.

His immediate thought was to go to Carla, but at this late hour, he suspected she'd be sleeping. The last thing he wanted to do was wake her up. She was already upset with him. He didn't want to make it worse.

As it was, he barely slept that night. It only took one phone call to destroy the trust that he'd built up with Carla. He wanted to believe it was their working relationship he was worried about, but he wasn't that good of a liar. He liked Carla a lot. She was easy to be around. And he could talk to her like no one he'd ever known. She listened to him and didn't try to force him to do this or that. Quite frankly, he'd really miss her if she were to disappear from his life.

He halted his thoughts. Had he really just admitted that? Even if it was just to himself, it was wrong. He couldn't let himself get attached to Carla. He refused to let her or anyone get that close, because he knew what it felt like when the people in his life walked away.

He'd intended to clear things up with her first thing in the morning, but she'd slipped out the door while he was in the shower. This couldn't wait, so he headed straight to her office. He needed her to understand that he took this arrangement as seriously as she did.

He arrived at Carla's office just after nine. He didn't wait for Carla's assistant to announce him. "I have to speak with my wife."

He opened the door and barged into Carla's office, not caring who was in there.

Carla's widened gaze met his, and then her eyes narrowed. "What are you doing here?"

He closed the door behind him. "We have to talk."

"No, we don't. You just need to make sure your girlfriend knows to stay away from you."

In that moment, he realized what was going on. Carla wasn't particularly worried about how Rose might affect their business arrangement. No, this was much more personal. Carla was jealous. A warm spot started in his chest and then spread outward. A smile tugged at the corners of his mouth at the thought of his wife being jealous over him.

Then it dawned on him how dangerous this all could be. Because if Carla took this marriage too seriously, it would mean she would be hurt when it ended. And it would end. He just didn't want her getting hurt.

"Rose has never been my girlfriend. The only one who thought that was her."

Carla's mouth gaped slightly. She promptly pressed her lips together. "She must have had a reason to think those things."

He vehemently shook his head. "Not from me." He didn't want to get into all this, but Carla had right to know since she was his, um…wife. And so he told her how Rose had claimed to be pregnant so he would marry her.

"That's awful. Who does such a thing?"

He rubbed the back of his neck. "I don't know. But I never want to go through something like that again."

"I don't blame you. No one should ever lie about something so important."

"Not only that, but I'm not planning on having kids."

Her gaze searched his. "Do you mean now? Or ever?"

"Never."

Carla stood and moved around her desk, pausing just in front of it. There was quite a length between them. "So where has Rose been all this time?"

Franco approached her, stopping just in front of her. His gaze searched hers, willing her to believe him. "She's been out of the country for work. She just got back. But don't worry, I told her I was happily married."

A warmth returned to her eyes. "You did?"

"I did. Isn't that part of our agreement? Putting on a happy front for everyone?" He needed to remind both of them that this marriage wasn't real.

Carla blinked, and it was though a wall had gone up between them. "Yes. Yes, it is."

And suddenly he regretted his words. He slid his hands around her waist. "But it doesn't mean we can't have some fun. I'm getting used to being your pretend husband. It has a lot of benefits."

And then he leaned in and pressed his lips to hers. It had been a spontaneous action. He should have thought it through. He was just about to pull away when her hands slid over his shoulders. They wrapped around his neck as she deepened the kiss. It would appear he was back in her good graces—her very good graces.

He'd always heard his married friends say that the fun of fighting with their wife was the making up. He never really understood what they'd meant until now. But this was definitely worth a restless night, because kissing Carla had never been better—

She jerked back and frowned at him. "What are you doing?"

"What am I doing? What are you doing? Because that kiss went both ways."

She stared at him, but he wasn't able to read her thoughts.

Knock. Knock.

"Come in," Carla called out.

"Excuse me." Rosa's tentative gaze moved between them. I thought you'd want to know that your nine thirty appointment is on their way up."

"Oh, yes. Thank you." Then Carla, looking like a no-nonsense professional, turned to him. "This is important."

He was being dismissed. He was a Marchello. People didn't dismiss him. But as his wife turned her back to him, he realized she wasn't like other people. So be it.

He turned and stormed out the door without another word. He'd thought she'd wanted him, but obviously he'd been wrong. He'd be sure to keep his distance going forward.

But once he was outside in the fresh air, he cooled down. She'd stung his pride, nothing more. Because in the end, she was right. It's better to keep things professional between them. He was foolish to think he could enjoy the benefits of their arrangement without emotional entanglements. After all, sex with Carla was never purely physical for him. It was so much more.

CHAPTER TEN

THEIR FIRST MEETING.

Their first official meeting as Mr. and Mrs. Marchello.

During the week following their wedding, they'd worked hard to bring their respective staffs on board with their ambitious plans for this venture. And to Carla's relief, the news was mostly met with enthusiasm. There were some of the old guard that were not enthused, as they'd been swayed by her father's derogatory comments about the Marchellos. But she was working hard to convince them to embrace this mutually beneficial partnership.

When she looked across the conference room table at Franco, she tried to see him purely as a business associate, but that was impossible as their steamy wedding night and the subsequent kisses were always at the edge of her thoughts. And that was making it really hard to focus on the task at hand—breathing new life into the Falco restaurants.

At one time her family's restaurants had been the place to be. Lines of people would form out the door as they waited for a table. Now business was steady, but it wasn't impressive. People didn't stand out on the sidewalks for an hour wait because they just couldn't live without a bowl of Falco pasta or their signature salads with house dressing or their fresh-baked bread with the flaky crust.

Her father had been so focused on expanding the chain that he hadn't slowed down to refresh the menu or update the original restaurants. She'd strongly urged him to reinvest in their current properties, but he was always talking about expanding the business.

Now at last she had a chance to implement her own plans. And her new husband was a part of that plan. She glanced over at him as he spread out his papers and set up his laptop.

"I've given your spices some thought," she said.

"I'm thinking that some special blends should be placed in the middle of the table in a caddy."

"How many spices were you thinking would be Marchello brand?"

"All of them."

"No." She shook her head. "I said we'd work together, but I didn't say you were taking over."

For a while they haggled back and forth. She remembered her father's warning about not trusting a Marchello. She'd made that mistake on their wedding night, thinking that possibly there could be something more to their arrangement than business, but she had obviously been mistaken. But it wasn't the first time she'd been wrong about a man. Her thoughts strayed back to her two-timing ex-fiancé, Matteo.

Her back teeth ground together. She shoved the troubling memories to the back of her mind. She had to stay focused on their business arrangement.

Franco wasn't interested in her. He'd made that abundantly clear on the car ride home... erm, to his place. But then there had been that kiss in her office. What was up with that?

She didn't know the answer. He confused her, and that was another reason not to get too comfortable in this new living arrangement. Everything was only temporary, except for the business. And she had to be extra careful that Franco didn't take over.

Franco expelled a frustrated sigh, crossed his arms and leaned back in his chair. "I don't know what you want from me. You keep rejecting my suggestions."

"Because they are—" She hesitated as she searched for the right word. She wanted something less bold but maybe she just needed to be up front about it all. "Well, it's boring."

"Boring?" When she nodded, he said, "I don't hear you coming up with any better ideas."

"I've been giving it some thought."

"And the only way for patrons to become familiar with our spices is to have them in front of them and to try them on their food."

"I think that's one way." Her phone buzzed with a new message from her assistant, wanting to know if she should order them lunch in. Carla responded that it was good idea.

"Okay. Keep going. What else do you have in mind?"

She thought he was agitated with her, but when she glanced up, she noticed interest reflected in his eyes. "I've done some brainstorming."

He leaned forward. "Let me see what you have come up with."

She closed her laptop. "I don't think so."

He frowned at her. "I thought this was a partnership, one where we shared everything including the good and the bad."

"But this is just some brainstorming. A list of ideas."

"Good." He reached for her laptop. "Maybe something on your list will help us."

She slid the laptop out of his reach. "I don't think you understand. This is a stream-of-consciousness technique that I've learned to do. It's just whatever popped into my mind at the moment." And she would feel too exposed if he were to read it.

He sighed and then he leaned toward her, resting his elbows on the table. "If we're going to work together, we have to be able to trust each other."

Her gaze met his. "I've been told to be wary of Marchellos."

"And yet you married one."

She opened her mouth and then promptly closed it without uttering a word. He was right. She just had to put her father's negativity and predictions of doom and gloom out her mind. He didn't know Franco like she knew him. He was an honorable man, who cared about his family and his family's business. Franco might not have any allegiance to her, but if he wanted his business to succeed, he needed her business to succeed.

With a resigned sigh, Carla opened her laptop and slid it across the table to him.

"Are you sure?" His gaze searched hers.

When she nodded, he pulled the laptop closer and his gaze perused her ideas—some were totally outlandish, others were too basic but hopefully there would be something in there that they could build upon, because time was ticking.

"I like this one," Franco said.

Since she couldn't see what he was pointing at, she asked, "Which one?"

He glanced up at her and gave her a sheepish grin that made her stomach dip. "Sorry. I forgot that you aren't looking at the screen with me. Why don't you move over here next to me?"

She wasn't so sure that switching her seat was such a good idea. There was something reassuring about having a big wood table between them. There was little chance of their fingers touching or their bodies brushing up against each other. It kept the match of desire from being struck and passion from flaming up and destroying this productive business relationship that they were struggling to form.

But it wasn't like they were conducting some heated affair. Sure, their wedding night was nice, but it wasn't anything spectacular—oh, who was she kidding? No one had ever kissed her quite the way Franco had done. When she was in his arms, she felt as though she were the only woman in the world.

Still, if she didn't move next to him, it was like admitting that his nearness got to her—that he had some sort of power over her. She glanced over at him as he continued to study her list. Her pulse raced as she took in his handsome face with his dark eyes, smooth skin and strong jawline. She was kidding herself, because nothing could be further from the truth. He did get to her. She just had to learn to ignore her body's heady response to him.

Against her better judgment, she stood. She moved around to the other side of the table and sat down next to him. She made sure to leave a respectable distance between them.

Franco pointed to the screen. "I think the first two are a bit out of our reach, and we don't really have the time to do something so involved."

"I… I agree."

"But this third one about incorporating the spices into your menu is a great idea."

"You like it?" The words slipped past her lips before she could stop them.

"Actually, I have our kitchen working on some new recipes that I was planning to use for promotional purposes, but if you'd like to use them in your kitchens, I think we could work something out."

She shook her head. "I don't know. We provide very traditional fare."

"I understand. Not all the recipes would work, but I think others could be modified so they would fit in with what your restaurants offer." He turned to her. "Would you be willing to give it a try?"

This would be the first thing they agreed on. She rolled the idea around in her mind. Besides the fresh paint, new decor and all new linens, perhaps the menu could use a bit of a facelift.

But she wasn't ready to let Franco see just how much the idea appealed to her. "I'll consider it, but I'd like to sample what you have in mind before I allow our kitchens to start working together."

He smiled and nodded. "I expected nothing less."

"Instead of just plain, solitary spices, what if we make some blends specifically for the restaurants?"

He nodded. "I like the idea."

She struggled not to show the surprise about him freely admitting that he liked her idea. Maybe this partnership didn't have to be so constrained. Maybe it would be all right to let her guard down a little with him.

The thought brought a smile to her lips. She had a feeling they could do great things together. And in the end, it would benefit both of them— um, their businesses, of course.

"With all the work we've already done independently, we're really ahead of the game," she said as her gaze scrolled down over her checklist.

"I agree," Franco said. "That's why I'd like to propose we roll out this promotion in stages."

"Stages?"

He nodded. "I know we have six months in which to make this plan a reality, but wouldn't it be more impressive to reveal our plans ahead of time and grow the anticipation?"

Carla leaned back in her chair while twirling a pen. What Franco was suggesting was so ambitious. They'd have to push themselves and their staff harder than they'd ever worked before. But was it possible?

"What exactly do you have in mind?"

Franco reached into a black leather-bound binder and pulled out a stapled set of papers. He placed them in front of her. "I propose we launch this venture in six weeks' time—"

"Six weeks?" She shook her head. "I'll never get everything done in time. I'm giving all our original restaurants a facelift. This timeline isn't possible in that short amount of time."

"Okay. But what if you were to complete one facelift—say, the flagship restaurant? Would that be doable?"

She gave it some thought. "I think so."

"Good. We can send in some photographers to document the facelift. It can be used in the campaign. Maybe something like…'we're spicing things up with Marchello Spices and a new look, but we're keeping the same dishes you've come to love generation after generation.'"

Carla grabbed her pen and immediately began writing.

"What are you doing?"

"Writing it down before I forget. It's really good. Maybe you're in the wrong line of work. If you ever want a second career, you might want to consider advertising."

Franco let out a deep laugh. He was so handsome normally, but when the worry lines smoothed, he was the dreamiest. And he was so close—close enough to lean over and kiss.

His phone rang and he answered it before she could put her thoughts into action. She told herself that it was for the best—but it didn't feel like it.

CHAPTER ELEVEN

THEIR PLAN WAS coming together.

Two weeks into their venture, and the basic structure of their PR campaign was in place. Part of Carla was exhilarated that her first major endeavor as the CEO of Falco Fresco Ristorantes was moving along so smoothly. But the other part of her knew that the sooner this deal came to its conclusion, the sooner Franco would disappear from her life.

The truth was she'd enjoyed this time with Franco. He brought out her creative side. He coaxed her to think outside the box...in more than one way.

Their lives had taken on a certain routine. Monday had become their day for collaboration, and the rest of the week they split up to work with their own staffs. When the weekend rolled around, she spent Saturday with her father, who refused to speak of her husband. Carla was all right with avoiding the subject of Franco, as her feelings for him were too confusing to explain.

But when Sunday came, they were expected at Franco's grandparents for dinner. At first, it had been awkward with Franco not putting off the wedding until they'd been back in the country. Franco insisted that he just couldn't wait another day to make her his wife.

He was so charismatic that she almost believed him. His grandmother grudgingly forgave him while his grandfather didn't give any hint of his feelings toward their marriage.

With the circumstances of their marriage sorted, his grandmother welcomed Carla with open arms. His grandfather, on the other hand, wasn't as friendly, but he at least acknowledged her presence, which was more than her father was willing to do for Franco. With each passing week, she'd grown more comfortable attending Sunday dinner—almost as though she belonged there.

However, this sunny Monday morning, she glanced across the desk anticipating Franco's reaction as he examined the mockup of their new menu. It had a colorful center insert introducing the new Marchello Spices. Her gaze took in his dark eyes to his smooth cheeks and strong jaw. And then there was his mouth. Oh, the delicious things he could do with it.

The longer her gaze lingered on him, the faster her heart beat. She should be focusing on these important decisions, but she found herself utterly distracted. What would it be like if they were a real couple?

Would Franco still be so willing to help her with the business? Or would he be angry that she was more focused on things at the office instead of spending time at home with him? Would he understand her devotion to her father and her need to do whatever it took to care for him?

She'd like to think that Franco would be understanding about all of it. After all, he was a workaholic just like her. And if he understood her career drive, then would he understand her other needs—needs that had nothing to do with spreadsheets and profit margins. Would he be more than willing to satisfy them?

It wasn't like they didn't have chemistry—they had that in spades. In fact, their problem was keeping all those sparks from erupting into a flame—

"Carla?" Franco's voice drew her from her fantasy.

"Um, what?"

"I said this looks really good."

"Really? You like it?" She'd been unsure if she'd chosen the right color combinations.

"Yes, I do. You did great." He smiled at her, making her heart flutter. "We make a great team."

Carla stood and moved to his side of the desk.

"Yes, we do. Just sign here." She pointed to the form that required both of their signatures. "And then we can get these off to the printers."

When she offered him a pen, their fingers touched. Every cell in her body tingled. Her gaze caught and held his a moment longer than necessary. Her heart tumbled in her chest.

In that moment, she had to wonder why she'd insisted on a platonic relationship. He took the pen and scrolled his name on the appropriate line. And then he turned to her, but she was standing a little too close and his shoulder brushed against her. She should step back, but her feet refused to comply.

"Shall we celebrate?" Her voice came out in a breathy tone.

Desire flared in his eyes. "What did you have in mind? Maybe an early dinner?"

"No. I don't want to wait that long."

He reached out, gripping her waist. "I like the way you think."

His mouth pressed to hers, making time stand still. And yet her heart beat wildly. It didn't matter how many times he kissed her, it always had the same intoxicating effects as the first one.

As he drew her to him, she willingly followed his lead. Her arms wrapped around his neck, allowing her fingertips to comb through his thick, dark hair. As she gave herself over to the moment, a moan of pleasure swelled in the back of her throat.

She was kissing her husband. Those last two words played over and over in her mind. It was so strange to know they had a piece of paper that said this display of affection was all right and encouraged. Not that she needed any encouragement.

She took over the lead and intensified the kiss. It was impossible for her to get enough of him. She pushed him back against the edge of the desk, ignoring the sound of pens and papers falling to the floor. Reality had no room in this moment. Her fingers moved to his tie, pulling it loose so she could get to the shirt buttons beneath—

"What is going on here?" The boom of her father's disapproving voice immediately chilled her blood.

She jumped back. Her heart stilled as she groaned inwardly. She couldn't believe she'd been caught making out with her husband by her father, of all people. Where was her assistant? Why hadn't Rosa headed him off? She knew Carla didn't like to be surprised by her father.

Carla smoothed her hands down over her clothes, making sure nothing was out of place. And then, with heat warming her whole face, she turned to him. It didn't seem to matter how old she got, her father had that effect over her.

Why was she acting like she was a teenager again, getting caught making out on the couch with her boyfriend?

She swallowed hard. "Papa, what are you doing here?"

His gray brows furrowed together. "This is a business office. I didn't think I had to explain my presence. So am I to presume this so-called marriage is real?"

Carla chanced a glance at Franco. She sent him an apologetic look as he straightened his tie. She'd never meant for this to happen. Of all the times for them to lose their focus on work and let the passion between them flare up and consume them.

With his tie straightened, Franco draped an arm around Carla's waist and drew her near. "Yes, it's a real marriage."

Franco's unwavering stare met her father's. It appeared there was to be a battle of wills. *Oh no! This is not good, not good at all.*

Carla pulled away from Franco's hold. She stepped closer to her father. "Papa, what did you need?"

Her father's gaze turned to her. "He's lying to you and you don't even know it."

"Lying? Lying about what?"

"Everything. This marriage. This business deal. When it's all over—when he gets what he wants—he'll leave you with nothing but a broken heart. He's a liar just like his grandfather—"

"That's not true." Franco's restrained voice held a thread of anger. "If anyone here is a liar, it's you."

Her father's gaze narrowed as his face filled with color. "I don't know what your grandfather told you—"

"He didn't have to tell me anything. There's proof. I know for a fact that you cheated."

"Is that what you've been telling my daughter?" Her father stepped toward Franco.

"Stop!" Carla stepped between the two men. There was absolutely no way she was going to let them come to blows.

And quite frankly she wasn't even sure what they were fighting over. It seemed that both men knew something she didn't, and she was so tired of being left out of things. Her mother had done it with her illness. Her father did it with the business. And now Franco had done it with the secret he knew about her father.

Her father continued to glare at Franco. "Then tell your husband to take back his empty accusation—"

"It isn't empty," Franco ground out. "I can prove it."

For the briefest second, surprise lit up her father's eyes. But in a blink, it was gone. It didn't matter. Carla had seen it, and she wondered about this proof.

She stepped up to her father. "Tell me it isn't true. Tell me I haven't been falsely defending you all this time." When her father didn't immediately respond, she said, "Papa, say something."

Her father stepped around her and approached Franco. "I'm telling you that if you hurt my daughter, you'll have to deal directly with me." And then her father turned to her. "And when you're in my office, I expect you to act like a respectable businesswoman."

He didn't say another word as he strode out of the office, leaving her speechless. She felt as though the ground beneath her feet had shifted.

Did he lie to me?

All this time she'd just taken it for granted that her father was an honorable man, who always spoke the truth. She'd have defended him until her final breath. But had she been wrong about him?

No. That is not possible.

But she'd caught a glimpse of worry in his eyes before he'd moved to confront her husband. She didn't know what to believe.

She wanted to go after him and have it out, but she resisted. She vividly remembered the doctor's stern warning about avoiding undo stress.

Hurt and angry, she turned to Franco with

an accusing glare. "How dare you speak to him like that?"

"Me?" He pressed a hand to his chest. "What about him? He's the one throwing around insults."

She crossed her arms and frowned at him. "And you're the one that kept egging him on."

"Why are you mad at me? He's the one that barged into your office—an office that had the door closed, I might remind you—and yet you're attacking me."

"Because you're strong and healthy. He's not." With each word uttered, her emotions rose, as did her voice. "He needs to be taken care of. He doesn't need you yelling at him—"

"I didn't raise my voice, but if he'd kept it up—"

"You'd what?"

Franco huffed out a breath as he raked his fingers through his hair. "Nothing."

"Oh, it was something, all right." She tapped her foot. "And I want to know what you were going to do if he hadn't left."

His intense glare met hers. If he thought she was going to back down, he had another thought coming. Because as fiery as their passion could be, it appeared their tempers ran just as high. "I wasn't going to just stand by quietly while he insulted me, my family...and most especially you.

I had to speak the truth. I'm sorry you ended up getting hurt. That was never my intention."

"Is that why you kept this secret all this time? Why did you let me make a fool of myself defending him?"

He glanced downward. "I know what it's like to have a distant relationship with my father. I didn't want to say anything to cause trouble between you and your father."

She paused as she took in his words. And suddenly the fire went out of her temper. But she refused to get swept off her feet by his chivalry. Still, she wanted to be sure she heard him correctly. "You were coming to my defense?"

He glanced away as he shrugged. "Yeah. Sure. I guess. Now can we move on?"

It wasn't the strong affirmation that she'd been hoping for, but it definitely wasn't a denial. "You were lying when you told my father there was proof, weren't you?"

She really needed him to say yes. Because if he said something else, that would mean what she believed about her father—being an honest, loyal and respectable man—wasn't true. And… and that just couldn't be so.

Franco turned his back to her as he bent down to start gathering the evidence of their moment of reckless passion. That exquisite moment seemed so long ago now. If her father had set out to drive a wedge between her and Franco, he'd succeeded.

"Franco, answer me." Her voice wavered ever so slightly with emotion. "Do you have proof?"

He didn't answer her as he continued to pick up papers and pens from the floor. Once everything was placed on the side of the desk, he straightened. And then he turned to her. "We should drop the subject. I shouldn't have said anything to your father. I'm sorry. It's just that he got to me."

"My father is good at pressing people's buttons. But that still doesn't answer my question."

"Does it matter?"

"It matters very much."

Franco blew out a deep sigh. "There's a video of your father cheating at a high-stakes poker game."

Her gaze searched his. Nothing in his demeanor said he was lying or in any way out to get her. Instead, sympathy reflected in his eyes.

She pressed a hand to her mouth as she gasped. It was true. Her father had cheated at cards and then publicly shamed Franco's grandfather by calling him a liar to friends and business associates alike.

Her vision blurred. How could he have done such a thing? The man that she'd looked up to her whole life—the man that she'd given up her dreams for—had lied to her. He had told her that her sweet, kind husband was a liar—he'd insisted on it—and all along he was the liar, the cheat.

Her heart ached. Her father hadn't respected her enough to tell her the truth. Did he think she'd stop loving him? That would never happen. But she was hurt and disappointed. A tear splashed onto her cheek.

The next thing she knew, Franco was drawing her into his embrace. He held her and stroked her hair. "It's okay. It was a long time ago."

Her tears spilled onto Franco's blue dress shirt. It was only then that she realized she was crying. She hated to cry. She wasn't this weepy person. She was strong.

But hearing that about the one person in her life whom she thought she could trust thoroughly had broken something within her. Maybe it was the childhood belief that her father could do no wrong. Maybe it was losing her mother so quickly and far too soon that had her putting her father up on a pedestal. Whatever it was, she'd never look at him quite the same way again.

Drawing on the strength she knew lurked deep down inside her, she pulled back from Franco. She swiped at her eyes that must be a smear of mascara by now. "I'm sorry about that."

"Don't be." His voice was soft and warm like

a giant hug. "I'll take any excuse to hold you in my arms."

Her gaze dipped to his lips. And then, throwing caution to the wind, she leaned forward, pressing her mouth to his. At first, he didn't move, as though he was totally caught off guard by her boldness.

As his mouth began to move over hers, she felt careless, reckless. It was as if by finding out her father wasn't the man she thought him to be that she no longer had to hold herself back and play by the rules.

"Hold that thought," she said. And then she lifted her phone and dialed her assistant. She sent her home early. Then she locked her office door.

When she turned back to Franco, his eyes lit up with interest. "Should I be worried?"

She kicked off her heels and slowly approached him. "That depends. What are you worried about?"

A smiled toyed at the corners of his mouth. "With the way you're eyeing me up, I have a feeling you're about to take advantage of me."

She felt freer than she'd felt in a very long time, which was funny because she was married and not free at all. And in this moment, being married to Franco was all right with her. "Do you want to be taken advantage of?"

When she came to a stop in front of him, he gazed deep into her eyes. "Oh yes, I do."

That's all she needed to hear. She once again tugged at his tie, loosening it. And then her fingers fumbled with the shirt buttons. This time there were no reservations, no doubts about her actions.

In this particular moment, all she wanted was Franco—all of him. She loosened two buttons before he swept her up into his strong arms and carried her to the couch. He laid her down and then joined her.

His lips pressed to hers. It was like a balm upon her broken heart. As the kiss intensified, she momentarily forgot about the lies, the pain and the disappointment. In this moment, she felt wanted and cared about. She didn't want this moment to end.

CHAPTER TWELVE

CARLA WASN'T GOING to be outdone.

Three weeks of working practically nonstop and they were making great strides. With all the pressing matters to be resolved, she hadn't had time to visit her father. She still phoned each day, but their conversations were short and stilted. However, she made sure to send over updates on this new venture with Marchello Spices out of courtesy.

Oh, who was she kidding? She'd purposely been avoiding seeing him or having any meaningful conversation. She knew the subject of the infamous poker game would inevitably come up, and she wasn't ready for what he would say.

Because even though she'd denied the truth as long as she could, she knew the one man she'd trusted most in this world had lied to her. But hearing him admit it…it would change their relationship forever.

When he called, she always rushed off the phone. And when he'd invite her over for dinner, she said she had work to do on her big project. She noticed that he was going out of his way to be nice to her, but she wasn't ready. Not yet.

She knew she couldn't avoid him or the subject forever. But she told herself that she'd deal with it when the time was right. She just wasn't certain when that might be.

Right now, she had other matters on her mind. In exchange for putting Marchello Spices in all of the Falco restaurants, Franco was advertising their restaurants on their website and print ads, as well as adding a "Now featured in Falco Fresco Ristorantes" to their spice labels.

Their joint staff had pushed for promoting their marriage as a marrying of the restaurants and the line of spices. And under normal circumstances it would be an ideal PR campaign with the two heirs marrying, but they both knew this marriage would soon end, and they didn't want their divorce to tarnish all their hard work.

The staff had been disappointed, as they'd already brainstormed all the ways their marriage could be used to promote their family businesses. Carla and Franco explained away their reluctance to make the campaign personal because the businesses involved more people than just themselves.

Monday morning, Carla had been up before the sun—in fact, she'd been up before Franco— and out the door. At every meeting so far, it felt as though he was always a step ahead of her. And that wasn't good.

This deal had been her brainchild. She should be the one leading the way through this new collaboration. As such, she'd called an upper management meeting. She'd told them she didn't care if it took overtime, she wanted new material for this collaboration from additional product placement to innovative advertising targeted at the young crowd. She wanted everyone to know that this wasn't just their grandparents' and parents' place to eat but a destination for first dates and engagements.

She didn't care what part of this venture it was, she wanted fresh ideas. And lately she'd found herself quite distracted between her sexy new husband—erm, her partner, and worrying about her father, who in turn was worried about her.

Carla glanced at the time on her computer monitor. Less than an hour and Franco would show up. He liked to show up early, looking all prepared, while she was scrambling to put out fires before pulling together her latest developments on the project. She seemed to think that people who showed up early didn't have enough work to do. She definitely had enough work to do and then some.

Knock. Knock.

She glanced up at her open office door to

find Stu Phillips, the head of publicity, standing there. The man was in his sixties. His white hair was trimmed short. His black-rimmed reading glasses sat low on his bulbous nose. His gray eyes peered at her over the rims. He still wore his dark suit and tie, even though a few years back she'd talked her father into implementing a business-casual policy.

In his hands were a stack of papers. *Oh, good. This is just what I need.*

Carla waved him inside the office. "I was hoping to have something to present at our meeting today. What do you have for me?"

"We've worked on some new labels for the spices." Stu was polite, but he wasn't overly enthused that she was now in charge. He was part of the old guard, personally hired by her father. "I honestly don't know why we have to change all our labels just because we're going to add a couple of spices from that Marchello company."

This wasn't the first time he'd voiced his complaint. He must have thought that repeating himself would make her agree with him. He was wrong. "You're doing this because I told you to."

"But when your father comes back—"

"My father will back my plans." Her unwavering gaze met his. "But in the meantime, I'm here and I'm the boss. So we're going to do this my way."

Redesigning the in-house labels perhaps wasn't

where she would have started. She'd have probably worked on the macro vision for this project and then worked her way down to the micro images. But she wasn't one to tell people how to do their jobs, so long as they got good results. "Let's see what you have."

She held out her hands for the printouts. He glared at her, and she mentally dared him to continue to argue with her. She wasn't in the mood to take any flak. She had more important things on her mind.

He wisely chose to hand over the papers quietly.

She glanced over the new labels, taking in the choice of words, the font used and the colors selected. None of it was what they'd discussed. They greatly resembled their current labels.

She set the pages on the desk and lifted her gaze to meet his. "Were you in the same meeting as I was when we discussed the new look?"

"Yes, but—"

"No buts. This is not what I want. None of this is going to work. Go back and do better."

His gray brows drew together as storm clouds gathered in his eyes. He hesitated to move as though he was ready to tell her that he knew better. He didn't. The truth of the matter was that he was costing her time—time she didn't have.

"You know what," she said, "I'm going to accompany you back to your department. We're going to review what I expect so there are no further misunderstandings. And definitely no more delays."

Not waiting for Stu to disagree, she got up from her chair and headed for the hallway. She didn't have much time before Franco showed up, but this was critically important to the launch of their plan. Franco would understand if she wasn't sitting here waiting for him. At least she hoped so.

He was early.

Franco liked to make it a habit to be early to meetings. He supposed that it was a bit of his grandfather coming out in him. He had been taught that a person who took his work seriously made time for it and didn't use excuses to explain being unprepared.

Promptness showed a person's character. He liked to think that his early arrivals showed everyone around him that he was very serious about his business and that there wasn't anything more important to him.

He moved with long strides down the hallway until he came to the outer area of Carla's office. They'd planned to meet privately before the committee meeting in the conference room. The inner door to Carla's office was open, but she wasn't inside. When he turned his attention to her assistant, she was on the phone. Rosa held up a finger, indicating that it'd just be a moment.

He backtracked into the hallway, not wanting to lurk about and overhear her conversation. He was hoping to catch sight of Carla. They'd missed each other that morning.

What had her up and out of the penthouse so early? He couldn't help but feel that it had something to do with their collaboration. Right now, it was the main focus for both of them, because they were both working within shorter time constraints. And lately they'd been hitting one stumbling block after another.

"*Signor,*" Rosa called out to him.

He stepped into the office. "Sorry to bother you. I was supposed to meet with Carla."

Rosa nodded in understanding. "She said you would be stopping by. She had to step out of her office for a moment. She said you could wait inside for her. She shouldn't be long."

"*Grazie.*" He smiled at the woman before stepping into the office.

He sat down in one of the black leather chairs facing her desk. He lifted his briefcase to his lap and pulled out some papers he'd brought to show her.

Carla's desk was filled with binders and folders, so he stood and walked around to place the printouts in the center of her desk where she could see them right away. As he turned away, he noticed the image of a spice container.

He recalled her mentioning that they were going to work on the product labels. He picked up the papers and looked over it, finding that it said nothing about the Marchello brand. If it weren't for the name of the blend, he would think this was an old printout, but Harvest Zest was a name for a blend that had been developed at Marchello. He and Carla had discussed that particular blend at length.

And yet as he flipped through the pages of images, they all had the Falco name in large letters at the top as though the spices were theirs. Franco's jaw tightened. This couldn't be happening.

Had he trusted Carla too much? Had she found a loophole in their contract? Was she planning to take their ideas and run with them on her own?

He'd trusted Rose in the beginning, and she'd stared straight at him as she lied about her supposed pregnancy. Unease churned in his gut. Had Carla just done that with their business arrangement?

His back teeth ground together. This couldn't be happening. And he had no one to blame but himself, because his grandfather had warned him that the Falcos were cheaters. Foolishly, Franco had thought it was just Carla's father that couldn't be trusted, but now he had to wonder about her, too.

Knock. Knock.

Rosa stood in the doorway. "Excuse me. Carla just called and asked if you'd meet her in the conference room."

Franco placed the papers back on her desk just as he'd found them. "Thank you. I'll do that. I just need to place a quick phone call."

"I'll leave you to it." Rosa closed the door, giving him some privacy.

He quickly dialed his legal team. He alerted them to his concern that Carla might try to write Marchello Spices out of the deal. He didn't like to think he'd married someone who would turn on him, but he couldn't afford to take anything for granted.

He still didn't trust Carla, even though his legal team had assured him there was no way she could cut him out of this deal. He wanted to believe them—believe in his wife. But he knew firsthand that the people you were supposed to trust the most were the ones that could let you down the most.

If it hadn't been for his grandfather always pushing for everyone around him to do better, would his father still be here? Still be a part of his life?

As a child, he hadn't understood why his parents had left. He'd decided way back then to focus fully on being the best CEO possible when he grew up. And his goal never wavered—until he met Carla. Now he wondered what it'd be like to share his life with someone he loved and trusted. Could Carla be that person?

His heart said yes, but his mind kept throwing up caution signs. He had no choice but to confront her about the redesigned labels he'd seen on her desk. He didn't want her to think he'd been spying on her, but he didn't see how he had any other choice.

He disconnected the call and set off down the hallway. The door to the conference room was ajar, and Carla was the only one inside.

She glanced up from her laptop. "Looks like we're the first ones here."

"We need to talk." He closed the door, giving them some privacy.

She shut her laptop. "It sounds serious."

"It is."

He cleared his throat. "How are the labels for the spices coming?"

She glanced down to straighten some papers. "They aren't ready yet."

He was waiting for her to explain the reason her company's name was on the label instead of his. "Anything I can help with?"

She shook her head. "I've got it. I've been working on it personally."

That just made it worse. Any thoughts of pursuing some alone time with Carla just fizzled away. If he couldn't trust her, he just couldn't let her get close to him.

He cleared his throat. "Why isn't the Marchello name on the in-house labels?"

Her gaze met his. Worry reflected in her eyes. "What are you talking about?"

"I saw the mockups on your desk. They look a lot like your current labels."

She sat up straight. "You weren't meant to see those."

"Because you're planning to cut me out of this deal and run with all of our ideas on your own?"

Her mouth opened as though she was appalled by his accusation, but he noticed she didn't immediately deny the allegation. Then her glossy lips pressed into a firm line as her eyes darkened with anger. "Is that really what you think of me?"

"You wouldn't be the first person in my life to put your personal interests ahead of your obligation to me."

All of a sudden, the flames of anger were doused and she looked upon him with sympathy. "Are you talking about your parents?"

He shrugged. "It doesn't matter. I just need to know that you're going to keep your word."

"I am. I promise."

He wanted to believe her. But could he? His heart said yes. But his mind said to be cautious.

CHAPTER THIRTEEN

"WHERE ARE WE GOING? There's work to be done."

The following week, Franco smiled at Carla's complaint. He guided his dark sedan along the roadway toward the northern Lake Como region. He had just seen the new in-house labels with the Marchello name prominently displayed. Carla had kept her word.

And now he'd planned a special field trip for them. They'd been working night and day ironing out the details of this collaboration. At times, it'd been intense. At other times, they'd played off each other's inspiration.

This venture was going to be so much more than he'd ever hoped for—bigger than any PR campaign that Marchello Spices had ever participated in throughout the history of the company. And he couldn't wait to reveal it all to his grandfather. It would prove to him once and for all that he was the rightful successor.

"Franco, you missed the turnoff to the lake."

"I know. We have a stop to make before we go to the villa."

"But I thought you said this was going to be a working weekend."

"It is, but today is so warm and sunny that I thought we'd work outdoors." He smiled as he thought of the special plan he'd put together.

"Outdoors? I don't think so. Now isn't the time to lose focus. We are so close to having this plan all mapped out. Then we just have to put all the pieces into action."

They already had quite a few projects in the works. Both of their companies had come into this agreement with plans already underway. Carla's company had the facelifts planned and in motion with the restaurants, while his company had worked on new spice combinations as well as recipes to highlight those spices.

But there was still one area where the two of them just couldn't come together—the advertisements for this new venture. Carla wanted to go with the tried-and-true ad segments with young people enjoying food in a Falco restaurant. She was eager to draw in the young crowd who would turn into lifelong patrons.

He, on the other hand, wanted to do something totally new to show the viewers, both young and old alike, that even though it was still their favorite reliable restaurant, there was something new lurking beyond its doors. They'd even had numerous PR teams pitch ad campaign after ad campaign. While they liked bits and pieces of the various ads, none were the full image they'd been hoping for.

But Franco had something in mind, and he was willing to gamble a day of work to play it out and see if he and Carla could agree upon one vision that they could take back to their teams.

"Just relax." He easily guided the car along the narrow, winding road.

She didn't say anything as she leaned her head back against the seat and stared out the window at the passing greenery. He hoped the crew he'd put in charge of this surprise wouldn't let him down. He'd given them very precise instructions.

Finally, their destination came into sight. Franco slowed the car and pulled off to the side of the desolate road near a white panel truck with the Marchello Spices slogan emblazed on the side.

"Where are we?" Carla sat up and looked all around at the empty field.

"This property belongs to a friend of mine."

Just then the men climbed into the white truck and with a wave pulled away, allowing a view of a table with a red-and-white tablecloth in the middle of the green field with the mountain range in the background.

"What is this?" Carla asked.

"It's my surprise. Come on." He climbed out of the car.

She joined him. Then he took her hand and led her to the table. He pulled out a chair for her. And then he sat across from her. In the center of the table stood a candle and some flowers. There was a slight breeze, so the candle remained unlit.

"This is—" she glanced around "—definitely different. But I don't understand what we're doing here."

That's when Franco reached into the insulated box next to him and removed two covered plates as well as wrapped utensils. "We talked about new dishes for the menu that utilize the Marchello Spices blends."

"Oh." She lifted the lid from the small china plate and found an arrangement of pasta and a side of a vegetable medley. "This is very impressive."

He smiled. "I hope you like the taste as much as the appearance."

"I hope so, too."

He poured them each a glass of sparkling water. And then they started sampling the food. There were numerous plates all done up with specifically chosen dishes as well as garnishments.

They ate and then compared notes. Some

were pretty good. Some dishes were not so good, but a few were exceptional.

When they'd finished eating, Carla said, "I think we've found our menu items. Of course, we'll have to run them by our focus group, but I can't see how they won't love them."

"Good. I'm glad to hear it. My group has been perfecting these recipes since before we started working together."

Carla took a sip of water. She glanced toward the road as a couple of cars slowed to stare before passing. "It looks like we're getting some strange looks."

"They're just jealous and wish they could have a picnic lunch like ours."

She turned to him. "Why did you pick this place? Why not eat at the villa?"

"Because I thought this might inspire thoughts for the ad campaign."

She looked all around. "You want to feature a field for the backdrop for eating our new dishes?"

"It's not just any field. It's picturesque, with the Alps in the background." He wasn't doing a good job of explaining his concept to her.

"I think I know what you mean," Carla said. "The food can transport you to a different place. By eating Falco Fresco with Marchello Spices, it can take you from enjoying the ordinary to experiencing something extraordinary."

He pulled out his phone and started making notes.

"What are you doing?"

"Well, it seems I'm not the only one good at thinking up slogans. I wanted to write it down before I forget."

"It's not that good."

"I think with your words and my vision, the ad campaign will be a big success."

She smiled at him, warming that spot in his chest. "I think we make a great team."

"I do, too." And he truly meant it.

"It's a good thing I thought of it." She sent him a teasing grin.

Carla got to her feet and pulled out her phone. She started taking photos of their surroundings. "I do like the idea of a table in the middle of a green field."

Franco cleared the table, placing their dishes back in the cooler. Then he texted his team to come back and pick up everything. His job here was done. Well, almost...

"Do you think our families will be impressed?"

"How could they not be?" She smiled at him. "You mentioned seeing your parents from time to time. Will either of them attend the reveal party?"

He shook his head. "My father never attends public functions, especially if they're about the family business. And my mother, well, I have no idea what she's doing these days."

Carla reached out, placing her hand over his. "I'm sorry. I shouldn't have mentioned it."

He didn't like her looking at him like he was weak and not as good as everyone else—the way he felt in school when there was a special event for his parents to attend and instead he either skipped it or brought his grandparents. And it didn't go unnoticed by his classmates, who'd make snide comments. He pushed the painful memories to the back of his mind.

Instead of speaking of his past, he asked, "You lost your mother, too. Is that why you let your father get away with so much?"

She glanced away and then nodded. "I'd been away at school when my mother got sick. She insisted they wait to tell me about her prognosis until I came home for the holidays. What neither of my parents anticipated was how quickly her disease would progress."

"So they lied to you?"

"They did. When I saw my mother again, she was so weak and sick." Carla swiped at the tears on her cheeks.

He'd thought he'd had a rough childhood, but at least no one had lied to him. No one ever said his parents would come back for him and his brother. No one was that good of a liar.

He glanced down where their hands were still

joined. This time, he was the one to give her a reassuring squeeze.

"I'm so sorry," he said.

"I feel like if I had known, I could have done things differently, which is silly, because nothing I could have done would have saved her. But I wasn't ready to lose her. There were so many things I wanted to say to her, things I wanted to ask and things I wanted us to do together."

"Like plan your wedding?" When she nodded, he said, "When you get married for real, your father will be happy for you, and your mother will be smiling down upon you."

The thing was, he'd started feeling that this marriage was the real deal. When he had business dinners, Carla was the first person he called and profusely apologized to for not being able to dine with her. The truth was he'd lost his interest in wooing new clients. He'd rather be eating on the couch while watching some comedy rerun Carla had picked out.

It was only then that he realized in the short amount of time they'd been married, they'd settled into a routine—a comfortable routine. Perhaps too comfortable. Definitely too comfortable. Because what would happen when Carla left? And she would leave.

"Enough about us." Carla's voice interrupted his thoughts. "We should get back to work. When we get to the villa, we need to go over the final party details for our grand announcement." She got to her feet and then turned back to him. "Are you coming?"

"I, uh, sure."

She smiled at him.

"What's that for?"

"You just surprise me. I thought your whole life was about work, but it's not."

"It's not?"

She continued to smile as she shook her head. "This is a prime example."

"It is?" He wasn't sure he was comfortable where she was going with this, because his work was what was most important to him. It was what he could count on—what he could control.

"You could have given me a presentation on all this." She waved her hands around at the serene field and the picturesque mountains. "But instead you brought me out here for a leisurely picnic."

He'd thought he was making a strong pitch— one she couldn't resist. But would he have gone to such lengths for any other business associate? The answer was a resounding no.

And that worried him. Carla had him acting out of character. And worse yet, he liked doing all these things with her. But he didn't do commitments.

CHAPTER FOURTEEN

IT WAS LATE, and she was tired.

There were pressing matters on her desk. But nothing that couldn't wait for another day.

However, there was one thing that had been nagging at Carla. The way her stomach constantly felt as though it was on a roller coaster. For the past couple of weeks, she'd been so busy putting the final touches on this big reveal party that she hadn't had time to stop.

And dinner, well, dinner usually came from a takeaway container. Even though she'd been pleasantly surprised to learn that Franco was an excellent cook, neither of them had been home long enough to visit the kitchen for anything other than a coffee to go. And so for the past several days, she'd blamed her uneasy stomach and consumption of antacids on her poor diet.

Moments ago, she'd heard a couple of women in the break room talking about one being pregnant. She momentarily wondered if that was her problem. She quickly dismissed the idea. There was no way.

And just as quickly the memory of their wedding night came back to her. Oh yes, it was possible. In her flurry of nervous activity, she'd missed taking her birth control one day. One measly day. Was that all it took?

Carla rushed to her desk and picked up her calendar. Yes, it was a paper calendar because phones were great and all, but sometimes she needed to see things in print. Her crazy schedule was one that she wanted laid out in front of her.

And on her calendar, she kept some personal notes. She religiously marked the first day of her period with a little star in the bottom corner of that appropriate day. Now she just had to locate the little star. Surely it couldn't be that long ago.

There was no way she was pregnant with Franco's baby. No way at all. Because that would definitely complicate things in so many ways.

She'd just flipped a page in her weekly planner when there was a knock on her open door. Why in the world had she left the door open? Now was not the time for interruptions.

"Hi." Gianna stuck her head inside the doorway. "Can I come in?"

Carla pushed away her day planner and waved her cousin into the office. She sent her a weary smile. "I'm surprised to see you."

As Gianna stepped into the office, Carla

couldn't help but notice how her pregnancy was already starting to show. Carla's hand instinctively moved to her still-flat abdomen. Would she look like her cousin soon—all round with a baby?

When she realized what she'd done, she glanced down, grateful that the desk had shielded her action. She didn't need Gianna asking any questions, because she had absolutely no answers. She didn't even know what questions needed to be asked.

The only question that came to mind at the moment was…was she pregnant?

"I wasn't sure you'd still be around." Gianna's voice focused Carla's thoughts on their conversation instead of the frantic, rambling thoughts floating around in her mind.

"I had some last-minute things to do." Her gaze moved to her open day planner. There were no stars on the exposed page. But her search would have to wait for a couple more agonizing moments.

Gianna arched a brow. "Is everything ready to go for tomorrow?"

Carla nodded. Though internally she felt everything was anything but good. In fact, if her suspicions were right, everything was so very wrong. "We're all set for the big announcement."

"And how's your father taking all this?"

"So far he hasn't acknowledged my husband.

All he can think about is how I married the enemy. But he's intrigued by the changes to the restaurants."

Sympathy radiated from Gianna's eyes. "I'm sorry. Is there anything I can do?"

Carla shook her head. "It'll all work out in the end. My father may be stubborn, but even he can't argue when presented with profits."

"I'm just so glad this is going to work out for you and Franco. You two make a good couple. Not only do you get along at home, but you also work well together at the office."

Did they work well together both in and out of the office? As she thought back over the last several weeks, she realized that in the beginning things had been a bit rough, but as time went by, they'd learned to complement each other. Where one was focused on the cost, the other was focused on the creative end of things. Together, they balanced each other out.

But if she was pregnant, would that balance shift? Would the alliance they'd formed shatter? Or would Franco surprise her and be eager to be her partner through this, too?

"Carla?" Gianna waved her hand in front of her face. "Where did you go?"

"Sorry. I was just distracted…wondering if everything had been taken care of for tomorrow."

"Then I should leave you to get back to your

work. I just wanted you to know that I have delivered the last of the prints."

They'd hired Gianna to photograph not only the facelift at the flagship restaurant but also the meal in the field just as Franco had imagined it. And Gianna's work was stunning. No wonder she was an award-winning photographer.

"Your work is awesome!" Carla stepped out from behind her desk. "Thank you. You did a wonderful job making the colors pop. It's almost like you could step into the photos. And you really brought Franco's image to life with the mountains in the background. He was so pleased when he saw the proofs. I'm sure he'll tell you when you see him."

"I kind of thought he'd be here with you."

"He had a last-minute business meeting. It seems the word is out about our collaboration, and his company is picking up a lot of new distributors."

"That's great!" Gianna smiled. "Well, I'll see you tomorrow."

"Yes. I'll see you then. Thanks again." They hugged.

And then Carla was once again alone in the office with her thoughts—her ominous thoughts. She closed the door before rushing back to her desk. She couldn't bear any further interruptions right now. She felt as though the world she knew was about to explode.

She had absolutely no idea how she felt about the idea of a baby. At this stage in her life, she hadn't even considered whether she was going to have a family or not. Instead she'd been focused on her career and taking care of her father.

She drew the day planner closer. Her gaze scanned the page again for the elusive star that appeared to be missing from page after page. *Where is it?*

Was it possible she'd forgotten to make the notation? Yes, that was possible. Right now, she was willing to grasp any reasonable explanation, but at the same time she knew the missing star hadn't been a clerical error on her part, because she didn't recall having her period in a quite some time.

She groaned. *This is not good, not good at all.*

She flipped through too many pages for her comfort. And then she came to the week of her wedding. She noticed now that she'd doodled on it with wedding bells. She kept going. And then two weeks before the wedding, she found the little star.

She groaned again.

This can't be happening. Not to me. Not now.

There was only one way to tell. She grabbed her purse and headed for the door. She had a pregnancy test to pick up on her way home.

Please say it isn't so.

* * *

The pregnancy tests were in her hand.

All four boxes.

Luckily Carla had taken her oversized purse to work that day. She stuffed the tests inside the bag. They barely fit. But there was no way she was leaving something this big up to one measly test. Whatever the outcome, she had to be sure. She had to be absolutely positive she wasn't pregnant. Though the more she evaluated her symptoms and the amount of time since her monthly, she was more and more certain she was carrying a little Franco or a little Carla. She inwardly groaned.

All she could hope was that Franco's dinner meeting ran late.

What was she going to do if Franco was home when she got there? She probably should have called him to see what time he expected his meeting to end, but she was worried he'd detect the worry in her voice. And then the questions would come one after the other. She just needed a little time to herself. A chance to take the test alone. Because if her instinct was right, she'd be in shock. A baby was not in her plans. Not now. Not ever with Franco.

As she pulled into a parking spot, she groaned when she saw Franco's car. What was he doing home so soon? Usually his business meetings dragged on and on. But then she realized he might have left his car at home and gotten a ride to dinner. That thought bolstered her mood a tiny bit.

She headed inside and took the elevator to the top floor. She slipped her key in the lock and let herself inside. She paused and listened.

She didn't hear anything. *Thank goodness.* She unbuttoned her coat. It was such a relief to be home alone—

"There you are."

Carla jumped. Her heart lodged in her throat.

Franco stepped into the hallway and smiled at her. "I was surprised to beat you home."

"You…you're here?"

"Of course I'm here." He arched a dark brow. "I live here. Remember?"

"I… I know." Heat swirled in her chest and rushed to her cheeks. *Act natural. Don't let him suspect anything.* "I'm just surprised."

She slipped off her coat and flung it over the bulging purse. The last thing she needed was for it to spill open.

Because there was no way she was mentioning any of this to Franco. If she ended up not being pregnant, he'd get worked up for no reason at all. And right before the biggest day of their careers just wouldn't be fair to him.

And if she was pregnant? Her stomach took a nervous lurch. Well, she'd deal with that hurdle when she got to it.

"Carla, are you all right?"

"Sure. Fine." She plastered a smile on her face. "Why wouldn't I be? Tomorrow is our big day."

"It's just that you look a little gray."

"Gray? Boy. No wonder you don't have a girlfriend with compliments like that."

"Excuse me. But I can't have a girlfriend because we're married." He sent her a flirtatious smile. "Remember? Or should I remind you?"

"No. No. I remember." She ducked around him, hoping to escape to her room.

"Carla, have I done something to upset you?"

She paused and turned to him. His concern for her feelings would have normally made her heart flutter, but not tonight. Right now, all she could think about were the tests in her purse.

"Not at all," she said, "I'm just wiped out. I'm calling it a night." She headed for her bedroom. "I'll see you in the morning."

"But—"

She kept going. She just couldn't keep pretending that everything was all right. And she was scared that he was going to figure out what was going on with her. Though the logical part of her mind said there was no way that he could guess. But Franco knew her better than any other man ever had.

Finally she closed the door behind her. She didn't have time to stop. She needed to get this over with—just like removing a bandage, it needed to be done quickly. She took one of the tests and headed for the bathroom.

And then the waiting began. She checked the timer on her phone. Barely thirty seconds had gone by. Not able to sit still, she paced back and forth in front of her king-size bed.

Her phone buzzed. She checked her messages to find a text from her assistant. It would have to wait. She couldn't concentrate on business right now. She couldn't think about anything but the test result. It had to be negative. It had to be—

Knock. Knock.

No. No. No. Not now.

"I'm busy," she called out.

"Sorry. I just wanted you to know I brought home some food for you. It can be reheated."

"Thanks. I'll be out later."

She could hear his retreating footsteps. That was thoughtful of him. Franco was a really good guy, but she distinctly remembered him telling her he didn't want to be a father.

She resumed her pacing.

Five minutes later, the timer on her phone dinged. The moment of truth had arrived.

She rushed into the bathroom, picked up the test and found it was negative. A big whoosh of air escaped her lips. It was over. She'd been worried about nothing.

She picked up the box to throw it away when

a folded piece of paper slipped out of the box and fell to the floor. It was the instructions to the test. She probably should have read it before she took the test, but she'd been so anxious. And she had read the instructions on the back of the box. But this slip of paper had so much more information printed on it.

Her curiosity prompted her to unfold the paper. She started reading. A negative test result could not be guaranteed to be truly negative. A future test could be positive as the pregnancy progresses. But a positive test was a hundred percent accurate. Carla frowned.

She continued reading and found the test was most accurate first thing in the morning. She sighed. There was more waiting. But if this test was negative, she told herself the next one would be negative, too. She was worried about nothing.

CHAPTER FIFTEEN

TODAY WAS A big deal. A great big huge deal.

This was the day they'd been working night and day toward for six very long weeks.

Franco smiled. All the worry, all the stress and all the sleepless nights crouched over his laptop had been worth it. Because he'd done something even his own grandfather hadn't been able to accomplish—he'd gotten Marchello Spices back into the Falco restaurants.

There was no bigger restaurant chain in all of Italy. And as their chain expanded beyond the Italian border, Marchello Spices would go along for the ride, expanding their demographics into other locations. The sky was the limit as far as Franco was concerned.

A smile pulled at his lips as he buttoned the collar of his crisp white dress shirt. The only thing that could make this better was if Carla was right here next to him. And yet she'd withdrawn from him last night.

After how far they'd come from being adversaries to learning to be friends to something he wasn't quite ready to name—now she was shutting him out. Was it because the hard work was over? Their plan was in motion. Was she afraid he was going to bail on their marriage now that they were revealing the first stage of their plan?

Nothing could be further from the truth. Because he'd signed onto this agreement for six full months and that's exactly what he was going to do. This wasn't the end, this was just the beginning of their successful alliance—business and personal.

Because as good as they were in the office, they were even better at home. In fact, these days he now looked forward to coming home to her. Carla made him smile and laugh. She was great company, even when they were just sitting on the couch together watching one of her romantic comedies that he'd previously avoided at all costs. Now he actually didn't mind the lighthearted movies or the way Carla sighed at the end when the hero proclaimed his love and kissed the heroine.

Carla had shown him a marriage that was centered around a friendly companionship. She'd shown him that someone could offer a friendly gesture without expecting anything in return. And he'd found himself eager to get up in the morning to see her smiling face. Because he'd come to trust her—to know that she wasn't going to run away when things got tough.

But he also knew he couldn't judge what they had now like it was a real marriage. Because there was no expectation of forever. No one had laid their heart on the line. There were no entanglements to keep them trapped in this marriage.

They were both free to walk away. Just the thought of having a choice to stay or go made him feel lighter. Maybe this marriage contract hadn't been so bad.

He stared in the full-length mirror as he straightened his blue tie. Blue for victory. Today was a victorious day.

He walked out his bedroom door and headed over to Carla's bedroom. He rapped his knuckles on the door. "Carla?"

No response.

He knocked again. "Carla, are you ready?"

Still no response.

Maybe she was in the shower. He headed for the kitchen for his cup of coffee, not that he needed the jolt of caffeine today. Adrenaline pumped through his veins. He'd been dreaming about this day for a long, long time.

When he stepped in the kitchen, he found Carla standing in front of the sink. "Good morning."

"Morning." Her voice lacked enthusiasm.

"It's going to be a great day. Are you ready?"

It was then that he noticed she was still in her pale pink robe that gave a teasing glimpse of her toned thighs. His gaze lowered down the length of her long legs to her bare feet.

She turned a worried gaze his way. "Are you sure your grandfather won't be at the party?"

"Positive. He said he wouldn't celebrate anything that involved your father—"

"Because if they ran into each other—" her voice wavered with emotion "—it wouldn't be good. It'd be very bad. And with my father's health condition—"

"Shh…" Franco pulled her into his embrace. As her head came to rest on his shoulder, he said, "I know you're exhausted. You worked so hard for this moment, but trust me when I say this evening will be amazing. The hard work is done. Now it's time to enjoy our accomplishment. Tomorrow we'll worry about what comes next."

Her arms snaked around his sides, pulling him close. The weight of her body leaned into him. And in that moment, everything felt right in his world. Maybe they didn't have to rush out the door quite so soon—

Before he could put his plan in motion, Carla untangled herself from his arms. She smiled up at him. "You're right. Everything is going to be fine."

"You know, we don't have to rush off to the office right now—"

"Yes, we do. We've worked too hard not to see to every last detail. I'm running a bit late, but you go ahead."

Disappointed that he was being chased away, he said, "It's no problem. I can wait."

She shook her head again. "You should go ahead without me. I'll be a while. I need my hair and makeup to be just right."

He approached her. "Carla, what's the matter?"

She turned to him and flashed him a big smile, but he noticed how it didn't quite reach her eyes. "Why would anything be wrong? This is the day we've been working toward."

He also noticed that she was a bit pale. "Are you feeling all right?"

She glanced away. "I didn't realize I looked so bad."

"No. It's not that. You're always beautiful." It was the truth. With her long hair clipped up with some loose curls framing her face that lacked any makeup, he thought she was striking. But it was the lack of color in her cheeks that had him worried. "It's just that you look a little pale."

She shrugged off his concern. "It's no big deal. I didn't sleep well last night. A little makeup and I'll be good as new."

He glanced down at her hands. He'd expected to find her drinking coffee to give herself a boost of energy after a night of tossing and turning, but instead he found her drinking milk. "Are you sure you're feeling all right? Because if not we'll have to figure out somehow to explain your absence from today's events—"

"I'm fine. Stop worrying. Now if you'll get going, I'll be able to get ready in peace."

He hesitated. He had this feeling there was something she wasn't telling him, but maybe that was just a bit of his old insecurities surfacing, because over the process of putting together this large and complex project, he'd learned that he could trust what Carla told him. Why should today be any different?

"Okay. Do you need anything before I go?"

She shook her head. "I'm good. I'll see you soon."

And with that he walked away. The door clicked shut behind him. Though there was a part of him saying that he should have stayed just to make sure everything was fine with her, the other part of him said to trust her.

He was right.

Everything was going to be all right.

Carla had taken comfort in his words. She really needed to believe that everything would be all right. She wanted to believe all the worry over her father's health and then taking part in this fake marriage was what had her body all out of sorts.

And now that she thought it over in the light of day, it sounded quite plausible. After all, last night's pregnancy test was negative. Today's test would be negative as well. She was all worked up for nothing.

She dumped out the remainder of her glass and placed it in the sink to deal with later. Right now, she had other matters on her mind—matters that had kept her awake most of the night. She had to know for certain one way or the other.

She rushed to her room and once again went through the process. This time she took three tests at once. She wanted an actual reliable result—something she could count on.

Carla lined the three tests up on the countertop and then set the timer on her phone. She'd never known that five minutes could last so long.

She had a lot of things she needed to do that morning. She didn't have time to waste. She should be choosing her wardrobe from her work attire to her little black dress for the big cocktail party, but instead she paced back and forth just as she'd done the night before.

Her phone rang. She let it go to voice mail.

Her phone chimed with a new text message. She ignored it.

A minute or so later, her phone rang again. She also let it go directly to voice mail. Work could wait. This could not. She felt as though life as she knew it was on the line. And once she got the results, positive or negative, life would not go back to the carefree way that it had once been with Franco. She felt as though their relationship had been altered, even if he didn't know it. This marriage was more than business—much more. But what did she want from it?

Ding. Ding. Ding.

It was her time of reckoning. She silenced the timer and then rushed to the bathroom. The breath caught in her lungs as her heart pounded. She picked up the first test.

Positive.

What? No. No. No.

She picked up the second test. Positive. Her heart was beating so hard it echoed in her ears. Her breaths came faster and faster. *This can't be happening.*

One last test. She picked it up. Positive.

By now her breathing consisted of short, rapid gasps. She felt dizzy and sick to her stomach. She sank down on the white tile floor. She put her head between her knees to try and keep the world from spinning madly around her.

She was pregnant with Franco's baby. How was she going to tell him?

CHAPTER SIXTEEN

THIS DAY WAS GREAT.

Carla was amazing!

And Franco couldn't stop smiling. The day had been a whirlwind of interviews and photo ops celebrating the new Falco-Marchello project. Carla's office had handled setting up all the PR, and they'd done a fabulous job. The conference room had been filled with eager reporters and plentiful cameras.

When he'd first had the idea of getting Marchello Spices back in the Falco restaurants, he'd just thought about getting a couple of spices back on the tables. But with Carla's help and vision, they'd gone so far from his basic vision to something with momentum.

This project had taken on a life of its own from general spices to carefully blended combinations exclusive to the Falco restaurants. To new menu items that utilized Marchello Spices. And finally to the new ads featuring that special place Franco had taken Carla for that very special lunch. Every time he caught a glimpse of Gianna's prints, he couldn't help but smile.

They did great work together. And his grandfather was wrong when he said that working with a Falco was a mistake. Carla had proven time and again that he could trust her. And though he'd been leery of the marriage in the beginning—okay, more like downright opposed to it—it'd worked out. They hadn't gotten too caught up in it. At least nothing that couldn't be undone without destroying either of them.

And he was going to see if Carla wanted to continue seeing him after the divorce. Because he just couldn't imagine his life without her in it. Every time he thought of her, he got this warm feeling in his chest. He refused to put a name to it.

Maybe she wanted the same thing—maybe that's why she'd tried a couple of times that day to draw him away for a private word. But each time she'd approached him, right behind her was a member of the press. They'd latched onto this story because it had a lot of history— most families in Italy had at one time or another eaten a memorable meal in the Falco restaurants, and the red, white and green Marchello Spices shakers had at one point been a staple in most households. So their reunion was something that touched many lives. There was a lot of excitement.

But now as evening rolled around and they were about to head into the cocktail party, he didn't see Carla anywhere. He was eager to find out if she'd had the same thing on her mind about them giving in to their rising desires. He really hoped so.

With a plan to seek out Carla, he started to move around the room. His progress was hampered by business associates. He pasted on a smile and shook hands, but all the while his gaze darted around the room, searching for Carla. Where could she be?

And then he reassured himself that there was nothing to worry about, as she probably wanted to make a spectacular entrance. That was something his stunningly beautiful wife could do without even trying.

When his gaze strayed to the door, he came to an abrupt stop. The breath caught in his lungs. He didn't so much as blink as his mind rushed to make sense of what he was seeing.

It was his grandparents. They'd shown up at the party. Sure, they'd been invited—it'd been a matter of formality—but his grandfather had blustered on about not stepping foot in a Falco building or celebrating this ill-advised venture. Was his grandfather finally willing to admit that he'd done something even his grandfather hadn't been able to do—make Marchello Spices relevant once more?

Once the initial shock had passed, Franco moved toward his grandparents. "Hello."

His grandmother beamed at him. "I'm so proud of you. You're finally living the life I'd always hoped for you—a sweet wife and making your mark upon the company."

"Thank you." He wasn't so sure what else to say. His grandmother didn't usually speak to him in this manner.

And then she did something so out of character for her—she stepped forward and hugged him. The simple gesture had a profound effect on him. Franco hugged his grandmother back. He blinked repeatedly—all the flowers in the room must be making his allergies act up.

When they parted, he turned to his grandfather, wondering if he felt the same way. His grandfather wore a noncommittal expression. "I still can't believe you're not only married to a Falco but also doing business with one. I told you they can't be trusted."

"And how many times do I have to tell you that Carla is different? She's not like her father. She's up front and honest. She'd never take advantage of anyone."

"Don't be too trusting." Just then his grandmother elbowed his grandfather, and not subtly, either. His grandfather cleared his throat. "But you've done a great job with the business."

His grandfather did something that Franco

hadn't been expecting at all—he held his hand out to him. When Franco gripped his grandfather's hand, he gave him a firm handshake.

Then the most amazing thing of all, he saw pride reflected in his grandfather's eyes. He hadn't known how much he'd been craving that until this moment.

He walked his grandparents around the room, introducing them to some associates from the Falco group. They stopped at the buffet table. The spread was all finger foods with Marchello Spices being prominently displayed as well as utilized.

While his grandparents perused the table, Franco's thoughts turned to Carla. He couldn't wait to share his grandparents' reactions to this joint venture. She was never going to believe it. Because the success of this venture would be a hollow victory without Carla to share it with him.

She was a mess of emotions.

And she was scared. Her world was imploding.

And worst of all, she still had to tell Franco. Carla had tried repeatedly that day to draw him aside, but there had been one interruption after another. She felt as though she was sitting on a powder keg that was about to explode at any given moment.

She was hoping by telling Franco sooner rather than later that he would take the news better. After all, how could he blame her when it definitely took two of them to get into this predicament?

And so she'd skipped out on a few media events that day, letting her trusted staff and Franco handle the countless questions, including the one about why the two brands had ceased working together years ago. No one wanted to answer that question, but the more they evaded, the more insistent the media became.

Instead she'd spent time closed up in her office, finishing up some final details. It was all she could do to focus. Her insides were twisted in a nervous knot. She had to do something to calm down, because she couldn't show up at the party all frazzled. Everyone would know something was wrong—especially Franco.

She needed something familiar—something to ground her. As a matter of instinct, she grabbed her keys and headed out the door. It was time to go home.

Because when all was said and done, it was the place where she'd been raised, and her father was there. She might be upset with him right now, but it didn't mean she loved him any less.

When she entered her father's living room, she found him on the couch. His brows lifted in surprise. "I didn't expect to see you today."

"I..." She searched for a plausible excuse. "I needed to take a break before the party."

"Everything's all right?" His concerned gaze probed her.

She nodded. "The project is running ahead of schedule."

"Maybe then you'll be able to slow down and eat a meal with your father."

"We'll do that real soon."

It was on the tip of her tongue to ask if that invitation included her husband, but she stopped herself. She didn't think she could keep her emotions at bay if she started talking about Franco.

"You must be excited about tonight. I've gone over all the information about this joint venture. I know I was totally opposed to it in the beginning, but now I think you've done a great job. And I couldn't be prouder of you."

His kind words broke the dam around her rising emotions. She blinked repeatedly, but a tear escaped and landed on her cheek.

Her father stepped up to her. "Carla, what's the matter?"

She shook her head. "Nothing."

"You don't cry for no reason. Tell me what it is."

She swiped away the tear and forced a smile to her lips. "You've just never said anything like that to me before."

"Said what? That I'm proud of you?" When

she nodded, he continued. "I've always been proud of you. And that's why I'm going to the party tonight."

"You are?" This was the first she'd heard of it.

"Of course I'm going." He moved to the hallway. "I already have my suit picked out." He motioned for her to follow him. "I just need help choosing a tie."

This was new. Her father never relied on her to make decisions for him—not about his wardrobe or any other part of his life. She didn't know what to make of it.

Still, she walked with him and then chose a wine-colored tie. "Are you sure about this?" Her phone rang, but she ignored it. "It's going to be a big evening, and I don't want you wearing yourself out."

"Do you need to get that?"

She shook her head. "I have staff to take care of any problems that might crop up. Right now, I'm more concerned about you overdoing it. Remember what the doctor said about you slowing down and taking it easy."

"I'm not an invalid. Just because you have taken over the company doesn't mean I'm going to languish at home."

She nodded in understanding. "That's not what I meant. I'm just worried about you."

He paused and looked at her. "Now you know how it feels to worry about someone and want to protect them when they don't want to be coddled."

Carla opened her mouth to say something, but the words faded. She wordlessly pressed her lips together. What was her father saying? That everything he'd done—from trying to stop her from taking over the CEO's position to his matchmaking—it had all been his attempt to protect her?

This was too important for her just to let slide by. "Are you saying you never wanted me to run the company because you were trying to protect me from something?"

He sighed as he sat down on a bench at the end of his bed. "I never wanted you to repeat my mistakes."

Maybe with him calm this was the right moment to broach the subject of him lying to her. "Are you admitting that you cheated at the poker game?"

With a deep, resigned sigh, he lowered his head. "Yes."

The one word was like a dagger in her heart. Her wonderful, amazing father whom she'd held up on a pedestal all these years fell back to earth with a resounding thud.

She struggled to speak as emotions clogged her throat. "But why?"

Her father ran a hand over his jaw. "It was a bad time in my life."

"Bad enough to cheat and then lie about it— lie to me?" She didn't know what he could say to make any of that all right.

"It wasn't that long after we lost your mother. I was struggling."

He was? "You never let on to me."

"I couldn't. I'd promised your mother that I'd make sure you were all right. But when you weren't around, I was drinking a lot. The more I drank, the more I gambled. For a while, it was okay. I was on a winning streak. But then the tide turned and every hand was a loser. I drank more and gambled even more, trying to win back what I'd lost."

Carla sat down next to her father. "Oh, Papa, if I'd known—"

"I didn't want you to know. I knew how hard it was on you losing your mother. It got to the point where I'd lost all my money. I had to get it back. I only had one thing left that was worth enough money—the business." His voice wavered with emotion as he stared straight ahead as though lost in his thoughts. "I was certain that my luck would change. It had to, but I wasn't taking any chances. I'd slipped an ace up my sleeve. I didn't think I'd need it."

As her father revealed the whole sordid tale, Carla struggled to keep her mouth from gaping. Her strong, proud father seemed to shrink in front of her eyes. She didn't know how to react.

She was a ball of emotions: anger at being lied to, disillusioned that her larger-than-life father was fallible like the rest of us and sympathy for him that he'd suffered in silence.

"In the end, being accused of cheating was the best thing that could have happened to me. I just didn't see it that way until now."

"Why?" Her voice was barely more than a whisper. She wasn't sure she wanted to hear the answer.

He blew out an unsteady breath. "Because accusations were thrown about and Marchello had no choice but to walk away—without my company."

"And yet you called him a liar?"

Her father's head lowered. "It wasn't my finest hour. I was so full of anger, and he became my target. It wasn't right, and I regret it."

"Then why haven't you apologized?"

There was a drawn-out pause. "It's not that easy. What would he think of me?"

"But Franco's grandfather already knows the truth, and there's a video—"

"There is?" When she nodded, he asked, "But then why did he just walk away? He could have taken everything from me."

"Not everything. You will always have me." She leaned her head against his shoulder and hugged him. "Maybe Franco's grandfather was a better friend to you than you ever knew."

Her father was silent for a moment as he considered her observation. And then he cleared his throat. "That was the moment I started to get my act together. But you have to understand that I made mistakes before the drinking and gambling."

"Everyone makes mistakes." She should know—she was carrying Franco's baby.

"Before all that I made the business the center of the world. I always thought there would be time for other things—like taking your mother to see the world. It had been her fondest wish, but then she got sick and there was no more time."

"I... I didn't know." Her mother had wanted to travel. And here she'd always thought her mother had been content to stay at home and look after her. She hadn't realized her mother had other aspirations. She wondered what else she'd never known about her mother.

"Your mother didn't feel a need to talk about it. She knew that eventually there would be time to follow her dreams. None of us expected her to get so sick so quickly."

The pain of her mother's sudden loss could still be felt after all these years. "And so you wanted me to get married and have a family because you wanted me to be like my mother."

"No. Though would that have been so bad?"

She thought of the baby she was carrying

now—with every passing moment, the idea of being a mother was becoming more attractive. "No, it's not bad. But why did it have to be one or the other? Business or a family?"

"Because your mother told me from the time you were little that you were so much like me. I, of course, didn't believe her. I saw her in you from your dark curls to your caring heart. But your mother was known for seeing things that I was blind to. And then without your mother around to watch over us both, I feared that her prediction was right—you'd turn out just like me—make my same mistakes."

She'd never known any of this. Her father had never opened up to her. He had always been the one to keep things close to his chest. But it appeared that his recent heart attacks had had a profound affect not only on her but on him as well.

Buzz. Buzz. Buzz.

Who kept calling her? She pulled her phone from her purse and saw Franco's name on the caller ID. He was probably calling to remind her that they were to have some press photos taken with some prominent people at the party, but it was just going to have to wait. This conversation with her father was too important to walk away from now.

She placed the phone back in her purse. "What mistakes?"

His tired gaze met hers. "I made the mistake of thinking that if I built a successful business, it would keep my family safe. I was so driven to make sure my family wanted for nothing financially that I missed the fact that I was no longer an active part of your or your mother's lives. I was absent for too many birthday parties and anniversaries." His gruff voice hitched with emotion. "I... I didn't want that for you. So I thought if you married and had children, you would see that there was more to life than just work."

"I never knew." Her mind rewound back to all the arguments they'd had over her marrying. They could have been avoided if he would have explained this to her. "Why didn't you say anything?"

"Because I knew you'd ignore my warnings. Your mother was right—you are stubborn, just like me."

Carla wanted to argue with him. She wanted to tell him that his worries were wrong—that she wouldn't have put her career ahead of everything else. Instead she bit back her denial, because ever since Matteo had hurt her in the worst way, she'd closed off her heart—she'd closed it off to Franco, too.

Instead of letting herself be put in a position of being loved, she'd focused on her career. It was something she could control. It had been the safe choice.

And now that all three pregnancy tests showed positive, she felt more vulnerable than she'd ever been in her life. How was Franco going to react to the news? Would he blame her?

She shoved aside the troubling thoughts so as not to get emotional again and have her father ask questions—questions like what was she going to do next? She didn't have any answers. It was all so new—so shocking.

She changed the subject. "Thank you for being honest with me. You don't have to worry. I promise to have a life and a career."

He reached out and squeezed her hand. "I just want you to be happy."

"I will be." She just wasn't so sure about her happiness in the near future. "I have to go get ready for the party. Are you sure you won't consider staying home?"

"Absolutely not. I need to go brag about what my amazing daughter has accomplished."

At least Franco's grandparents wouldn't be there. He had been quite certain his grandfather would be too stubborn to go to a party and acknowledge Franco's accomplishment.

She hugged her father. "I'll see you later. And if you change your mind and decide to stay home, I won't be upset. Just call me. I'll keep my phone on me."

"Stop worrying. I'll be fine."

And then Carla was gone. As she checked the time, she realized she'd spent more time with her father than she'd intended. And now she was late for the party.

As for telling Franco the news about the baby, well…it'd waited all day, so it could wait until tomorrow. Because the party was no place to tell him the news. And looking back on earlier today, it hadn't been the time to tell him, either. It's just that she'd been in shock and her first thought was to tell Franco.

But waiting until the morning wasn't going to change the test results. As the instruction sheet had told her, a positive result was definitely positive. What was Franco going to say now that their fake marriage had become very real, with real consequences?

CHAPTER SEVENTEEN

Where was she?

Franco had slowly worked his way around the room, twice over, and there was still no sign of Carla. He'd even tried her phone a couple of times. Every time, it had gone directly to voice mail. What was up with that?

Was she avoiding him? He didn't think so. It's not like they'd had a fight or anything. Sure, she'd been a bit more distant in the last day or so, but that was probably just due to exhaustion.

But none of that explained why he hadn't found her yet. He'd stopped to ask her assistant, Rosa, but she hadn't heard from her in the past hour or so, since she'd left the office. He recalled Carla's pale complexion that morning. Perhaps she was sick. He was about to leave and go to the apartment to see if she was right.

As he headed for the door, Carla entered the room. He took long strides toward her. "Where have you been?"

She didn't look at him as she smiled at the passing guests. "I had to check on my father."

"Is something wrong?"

"No. I just wanted him to know that I would be fine if he stayed home."

He was relieved to hear that nothing was wrong with Carlo. Not that he had any warm feelings toward the man who had lied about him and his family all these years, but Carla loved him dearly and what was important to her was important to him—

Wait. Had he just thought that? While Carla paused to say hello to the CEO of an up-and-coming tech company, Franco realized just how important Carla had become to him.

When Carla was free again, he knew this was his opportunity to draw her aside. He placed a hand on her upper arm to gain her attention. When she paused and looked up at him, he asked, "Can we speak now?"

Her gaze met his, but her emotions were closed off to him. "Not now. It's a party."

"I know something is bothering you. Does it have to do with the launch?"

She shook her head. "Everything is on track."

"Then if it's not business, it has to be something to do with me." As someone passed closely by them, he quieted down and forced a smile to his face. "What have I done?"

Carla turned a smile in his direction—a smile that didn't reach her eyes. "This isn't the place."

Just then a flash went off in their faces. He'd forgotten about the media photographers covering the party. Franco wished they'd give them some privacy.

When Carla set off again, he fell in step with her. "But you were the one that insisted we speak earlier. I'm ready now."

She came to an abrupt halt and turned to him. This time there was anger reflected in her eyes. In a hushed voice, she said, "And I'm supposed to drop everything because suddenly you've got time in your schedule for me? I don't think so."

He stifled a frustrated groan. "You took that out of context. I'm sorry I was busy earlier. You know how fast everything is moving."

Just then a reporter approached them. The woman's face was perfectly made up, and not a hair was out of place. "Do you have time for a few questions?"

"We were just about to go take care of something," Franco said.

"But it can wait a moment or two." Carla flashed the reporter her fake smile. "What would you like to ask?"

"Would you mind if I record this?" She held up her phone. "I just want to make sure I get my facts right when I go to write up the story."

Carla nodded. "Of course."

"You two have made quite the stir this year. First your sudden marriage. Where was it that you tied the knot?"

Carla spoke up first. "It was at Franco's country estate in Lake Como."

"That must have been so romantic. You know, to be swept off your feet and a secret wedding and all."

"It was sudden, but we both knew what we wanted." Carla elbowed him. "Isn't that right, Franco?"

He was still pondering what Carla had on her mind. Whatever it was, it wasn't good. Worry seeped into his bones as he pasted on a fake smile to match Carla's. But whatever was wrong, he would fix it.

He slipped an arm around her waist and pulled her closer, just like happy newlyweds would do. "We just couldn't wait to be husband and wife."

"You two always look so happy, so in love. So what's it like to work with your spouse?"

"It's been great," Carla said. "Franco is great at coming up with solutions for tricky problems."

"And Carla is great with concepts and tie-ins."

The reporter smiled and nodded. "This sounds like the beginning of many successful collaborations."

"I don't know," Franco said with hesitancy.

"What he means is that we haven't gotten that far. We're just on the eve of launching this new campaign in all the Falco restaurants."

The reporter nodded in understanding. "And what about on a personal front? Will there soon be any additions to your family?"

Franco didn't hesitate to answer. "No. We're happy just the way we are."

When Carla didn't echo his sentiments, he glanced at her. Her face filled with color. "We haven't discussed having children."

It was true. They'd never once talked of having their own children. Still, her answer was definitely not an affirmation of his words. It was not the answer he'd been expecting. And now there was this agonizing suspicion swirling around in is mind.

The breath caught in his throat. Was she pregnant?

For a moment, it felt as though the floor had gone out from under his feet and he was hanging over an abyss. This couldn't be happening. Not to him. He'd always been so cautious—so very careful—until Carla.

Why had he instinctively trusted her? It wasn't like this was his first go-around with an unplanned pregnancy. At least the first time with Rose it'd all been a ruse to get him to marry her. But Carla wasn't like Rose. She wouldn't intentionally get pregnant. Would she?

"I appreciate you both taking a moment to speak with me." The reporter's voice jarred him from his frantic thoughts. "Our readers will be anxiously waiting for word of a little Falco-Marchello to carry on such a delicious merger. Now I'll let you get to your other guests."

When the reporter moved on, Carla tried to slip away, too. But Franco was hot on her trail. He leaned over and whispered in her ear, "We need to talk now."

Just then Carla's assistant, Rosa, approached them. Franco groaned inwardly. Why did they have to be at a party, of all places? Trying to find just a moment alone was virtually impossible.

This was his fault. He should have insisted on making time to speak with Carla earlier in the day—when they could have had this conversation in private, without worry of being interrupted.

Because what he was thinking right now just couldn't possibly be true. There was no way Carla could be pregnant. But he also knew she could be pregnant. It wasn't like they hadn't enjoyed their marital benefits.

But in the beginning, Carla had insisted she took care of birth control. He'd believed her. Had he been too quick to believe her? Was it possible she'd lied to him? For what purpose? Was she that anxious to have a family that she'd do it at any cost?

With every outlandish thought that came to mind, his heart beat faster. His blood pressure had to be creeping into the red zone.

Desperate for a moment alone with Carla, he turned to her assistant. "Rosa, could you cover for us for a moment?"

"Um…sure." Worry reflected in her eyes. "You aren't leaving, are you?"

"No," Carla said firmly. "There's not a chance we'd miss out on this big night."

"Something came up and I need to discuss it with Carla. No big deal."

Rosa nodded in understanding. "I'll see to things."

"We'll just be in the hallway." Carla pointed to where they'd be.

And then Franco slipped his arm around his wife's slim waist as they made their way toward the doorway that led to the back entrance to the building. He hoped it would give them the privacy they needed. Because he needed to hear Carla say that she wasn't pregnant. She just couldn't be pregnant.

What were the chances of that happening? The odds have to be minuscule. Right?

Once in the vacant hallway with the door closed behind them, Carla turned on him. "What are you doing?"

"What am I doing? What are you doing telling a reporter that we might have children?"

Her face was devoid of color. "That's not what I said. I said—"

"I know what you said. What you didn't say was that we aren't having children, not now, not ever." He paused, waiting for her to agree. Instead an ominous silence filled the void. "Carla?"

Her gaze was cast downward. "We should get back to the party."

"Not before we clear this up." His gut knotted as bile inched up his throat. "Carla, what did you try to tell me earlier today?"

"It can wait."

"No, I don't think it can." It seemed as though she couldn't work up the courage to say it, so he would have to do it for her. "Carla, are you pregnant?"

Her gaze met his. There was a whole host of emotions reflected in her eyes, from fear to anger. She didn't say a word. She didn't have to. It was written all over her pale face.

And then she wordlessly nodded.

His heart fell. His head started to spin. *This can't be happening.* This was never supposed to happen. And yet it had happened, and he had no idea what to do about it.

No wonder she hadn't wanted to tell him. She knew he never wanted a family. But with Carla, it seemed like one thing always led to another. They'd started out as in-laws, which led to chemistry on the dance floor at his brother's wedding. That had led to a business dinner. From there she'd proposed a deal that he just couldn't turn down. A fake marriage had led to a very real wedding night. That night had led to him seeing her not as one of those Falcos—the ones that had lied—no, instead he found her to be a caring, loving and generous woman. And now he didn't know what to think about any of this. He couldn't even formulate any words—

The door burst open. Rosa rushed up to Carla. "Carla, you have to come quick."

"What is it?" Carla's voice echoed her concern.

"It's your father—" and then Rosa looked at him "—and your grandfather. They've gotten into a very loud and contentious argument in the middle of the party. It's a disaster."

"Oh no!" Carla turned an accusing stare at him. "You promised your grandfather wouldn't be here."

She didn't wait for him to explain as she rushed in the door. He'd meant to tell her about his grandparents' unexpected appearance, but when he'd grown worried about her unexplained absence, it'd slipped his mind.

Franco was right behind her. This night was supposed to be so perfect, so amazing, but it was turning into a disaster.

The sound of angry male voices boomed

through the room. It was the first time the two men had confronted each other since the cheating episode. It appeared that time had not lessened their anger toward the other.

Carla worked her way through the thickening crowd as a number of people pulled out their phones to film the devolving event. Franco's own personal nightmare was going to have to be put on hold until they separated the men.

"Liar!"

"Cheat!"

At last, Carla stepped inside the circle. "Papa, stop."

"I…" Carlo Falco stopped speaking. "I…" Then he clutched his chest before collapsing to the floor.

A horrified cry erupted from Carla's throat. She knelt by her father's side. Franco grabbed his phone and called for an ambulance. It seemed like forever until he'd answered all the operator's questions. Yes, Carlo was still breathing. No, he wasn't conscious.

Franco knelt next to Carla. Time moved slowly. He'd never felt so helpless in his life. Carla held her father's hand as she pleaded with him to hold on. The desperation rang out in her voice.

And when Carla finally turned her big brown eyes to Franco as the unleashed tears streamed down her cheeks, he felt as though his heart had been torn in half. He would do anything to fix this for her, but he didn't know how.

"He's going to be okay." Franco didn't know that, but he certainly wanted to believe it.

Before Carla could say anything, the crowd parted and the paramedics rolled a gurney into the room. They stepped back, giving them room to work. It took a few minutes to take his vitals and hook him up to oxygen.

Franco reached out to wrap his arm around Carla's waist, giving her his shoulder to lean on, but she wordlessly pushed his arm away. He didn't like it, but he understood that she needed to focus all her thoughts and energy on her father.

When they lifted the stretcher with her father, Franco said, "I'll get my car and drive you to the hospital."

"No." Carla turned to him with more anger than he'd even known she was capable of feeling, and it was all aimed at him. "You stay here. You aren't welcome at the hospital. This is all your fault. You and me, we're over. My attorney will send over the papers."

Each of her words were like arrows slamming into his chest. His fault? What? How?

By the time he was able to translate his thoughts into words, she was gone. And he'd never felt more alone in his entire life.

How had things been so right, so promising

one moment and then so wrong the next? Now what was he going to do? His wife didn't want him in her life, and they had a baby on the way. It felt as though he was reliving his parents' nightmare.

They'd both married for the wrong reasons, and then they'd both complicated matters with an unexpected pregnancy. He raked his fingers through his hair. What was he supposed to do now?

CHAPTER EIGHTEEN

SHE'D NEVER BEEN so scared.

Carla couldn't remember exactly what had happened between her admitting to Franco that she was pregnant until she watched her father being loaded into the back of an ambulance. She vaguely recalled being furious with Franco but not her exact words.

She paced back and forth in the hospital waiting area. What was taking the doctors so long? She'd begged them to let her stay, but they'd insisted it was protocol for her to stay in the waiting area until they'd done their initial workup.

Please let him be okay. Please let him be okay.

She kept repeating the silent prayer over and over in her mind. With her head down, she kept moving. She couldn't sit still. She was filled with pent-up anxiety.

A hand touched her shoulder.

She came to an abrupt stop and turned. She expected to find the doctor in his white coat, but instead it was her cousin. Gianna's face reflected her own worry.

They wordlessly hugged each other. Part of her wished that it was Franco holding her, but she had too many conflicting emotions where he was concerned. And she couldn't deal with him right now. It was just too much.

When they pulled apart, Carla swiped at her eyes. Gianna guided her over to one of the orange chairs. "Sit down. You look exhausted."

"I'm fine." She didn't feel fine. She felt as though her life was being pulled apart at the seams.

"Have you heard anything?"

Carla shook her head. "They threw me out and told me to wait here."

Gianna reached for her phone. "Do you want me to call Franco?"

"No."

Gianna slipped the phone back in her purse. "Okay. What's going on?"

"This whole thing is my fault. I know I blamed Franco, but I shouldn't have. This whole marriage and business venture was my idea. I knew about the bad blood between my father and Franco's grandfather, but did that stop me? No. I'm the one who should be blamed. If anything happens to my father, it's all on me."

"Whoa. Slow down. Start at the beginning."

And so Carla did exactly that. Her father's

matchmaking, her plan to take care of him and then the marriage contract—it all came tumbling out. She even briefly mentioned their wedding night and now its complications.

"You're pregnant?" Gianna's excited voice came out loudly.

"Shh…" Carla glanced around to make sure there was no one around to overhear. "Yes, but it's the very last thing Franco wants."

"You told him?"

Carla nodded. "Right before my father collapsed."

"And he said that he didn't want the baby?"

"No. But he'd previously told me about his childhood and how he never planned to marry or have a family. He doesn't want to repeat his parents' mistakes."

"When did he tell you this?"

"A while ago."

"Maybe things have changed since then. He said he didn't want to marry, but he sure looks happy these days. Even Dario mentioned that he'd never seen his brother happier."

This was all news to Carla. "I don't know. He's probably just happy about our business venture coming together."

"No. I've seen the way he looks at you. It isn't the way a platonic business associate looks at the other. He looks at you like you're a double chocolate cupcake that he can't wait to devour."

Heat filled Carla's cheeks. "He does not."

"Oh, but he does. And I've seen the way you look at him when you think no one notices. You are crazy for him. It's the reason I never questioned your quickie wedding. I figured it was love at first sight. Or maybe second sight."

Was that true? Did he love her? And if he did, did it change things between them? Would he still love her even if she was carrying the baby he never wanted?

That evening couldn't have gone any worse.

Franco took one look at his grandfather's pale, drawn face and knew he was in no condition to drive. Franco and his brother had helped their grandparents into their car. His grandmother never did like to drive, so he drove them home. Dario followed them in his car.

As he drove out of the city, he just couldn't help but think about how things had looked so promising one moment and then in the next his world had come crashing in around him.

A baby.

He was going to be a father.

In that moment, he promised himself that he wouldn't be like his father, who was constantly avoiding his responsibilities. If it wasn't for his grandfather, he might not know what it was to have a father—how to be a father. Franco was going to be there for his child in every way possible. No one would drive him away.

When holidays and birthdays rolled around, he'd be there with an armful of gifts and a big smile. He would let his child know how much they meant to him.

He would do for his child everything that he'd wanted his parents to do for him, but instead they'd been too wrapped up in their own world—in their own problems—to see that their two little boys had been utterly and totally forgotten.

"Franco." His grandmother's concerned voice interrupted his thoughts. "Franco, you missed the turn."

He blinked. His gaze took in his surroundings, and he realized his grandmother was right. "I'll just circle back around. No big deal."

"Something is on your mind. It's your grandfather, isn't it?"

His grandfather was sitting quietly in the back seat for the first time since Franco had known him. A glance in the rearview mirror showed his grandfather with his arms crossed over his chest as he stared out the window. Franco thought for sure he'd have a few disparaging words to say about Franco missing the turn, but he continued to be mute.

Returning his gaze to the road, Franco thought

about his grandmother's question. "Actually, I was thinking about my father."

"Oh." She didn't like to talk about her son. The pain was always evident in her eyes when his name was brought up, and so Franco had learned to avoid the subject all together.

But today was different. All the skeletons in the closet and the ghosts that had been swept under the rug were going to be aired out—the light shined on them. Maybe that was the problem with their family. Maybe they avoided the tough subjects too often. Instead of the silence helping, it was hurting them.

Now that both he and Dario were about to be fathers, they didn't have the luxury of ignoring the past. They had to learn from it if they hoped to do better by their children.

He eased the car into the drive and parked in front of the massive villa. This subject could wait until they were inside.

He jumped out and opened both car doors for his grandparents. As they got to their feet, he noticed that they both looked as though they'd aged considerably since the confrontation at the party.

Once inside, Dario joined them. "Well, that's certainly going to be in the news tomorrow. I'm guessing that's not the headline you were hoping for."

Franco paced back and forth, raking his fingers through his hair. Then he stopped and faced his grandfather. "Why did you have to pick today of all days to change your mind and show up?"

"It's my company." His voice boomed in the large foyer.

"It was your company," Franco corrected him. "Remember, you're retiring."

"He's right," Nonna agreed. "You can't keep running the company forever. It's time you let Franco take over."

His grandfather's lips pressed into a firm line as a muscle in his cheek spasmed.

"I know that you never thought I lived up to this image you had of me." Franco's voice shook with frustration. "I've tried and tried to make you proud of me, but I'm done. I just can't do it anymore. You can keep the company. I quit."

"What…what?" For the first time ever, his grandfather looked to be at a loss for words. "But you can't."

"Oh, I can and I am." As he swung around to walk out the door, he caught the grin on his brother's face.

It seemed like not so long ago that Dario had had a similar conversation with their grandfather—then, Franco hadn't been able to understand how he could just walk away from his legacy. It'd taken a bit, but now he finally understood.

"Wait," Nonna called out. When he turned

to his grandmother, she said, "Don't go." Then she turned to his grandfather. "I've been quiet for too long. I thought you knew what you were doing where the boys were concerned, but you've gone too far now. Don't let him walk away. Not like this."

Nonno shook his head. "Let him go."

"No." His grandmother's voice brooked no argument. "Fix this. I won't lose yet another member of this family. I let you drive away our son."

"He wasn't strong," Nonno said. "He wouldn't stand up for himself. He always wanted to take the easy way out of everything."

"Maybe if you hadn't pushed him so hard, he'd have figured it all out."

"You blame me for him leaving?"

"I do. And I won't stand for it. Not again. Franco belongs at the helm of the company. He has earned the right to continue running it the way he sees fit." Nonna glared at his grandfather. "And if you don't step aside, don't bother coming to bed tonight or any other night." She turned and stormed away.

His grandmother had stolen all of Franco's thunder. She'd left him utterly speechless. He'd never seen her so angry. When he gathered himself to lift his sagging jaw, he glanced over at his grandfather, who appeared to have lost his ability to speak as well.

Franco had always taken his grandmother's

silence to mean that she agreed with everything his grandfather said and did. It appeared that wasn't the case. He was relieved that she'd finally spoken up, but he couldn't help but wish that she'd done it much sooner.

Franco hesitated, waiting to see if his grandfather would say anything. The silence stretched on. It went on too long. Franco continued toward the door.

"Wait," Dario said.

Franco didn't want to wait. Turning his back on his grandfather wasn't easy. Even if the man wasn't the easiest person to care about, he still loved him. But he couldn't just walk out on his brother, who'd always had his back. Through everything, they'd been there for each other.

Franco smothered a frustrated sigh and turned back. "It's not going to work," he said to his brother. "He's too stubborn to listen to anyone—"

"That's not true." Nonno's voice wavered, as though he wasn't quite certain.

Both brothers turned to their grandfather. His shoulders were slightly slumped as worry lines bracketed his face. It was though he'd aged right before him. Franco had never seen his grandfather anything but strong and assured. He didn't look like either of those things right now.

"You don't understand," their grandfather began. "You didn't know your father—"

"Let's sit down and talk." Dario moved toward the living room and glanced over his shoulder to make sure both men were following him.

Their grandfather fell in step behind Dario. Franco still hadn't moved from his spot near the door. He wasn't so sure there was anything his grandfather could say at this stage to change his mind about remaining a part of this family.

But then his gaze connected with his brother's. Dario nodded toward the living room. He could see in his younger brother's eyes that he was pleading with him not to walk away. It was so funny how things had flip-flopped between them.

Not so long ago, it was he who had coerced his brother into attending the family's Sunday dinner after he'd broken up with his now wife. And Franco couldn't help but wonder if he hadn't somehow been instrumental in getting those two back together—but as soon as the thought came to him, he dismissed it. Because it was perfectly obvious to anyone who saw Dario and Gianna that they belonged together. Even without him, they would have found their way back to each other.

But this talk didn't have anything to do with romance. It was about something much deeper—the fracture of his family. He'd always told himself that it was all in the past and to keep looking forward. But if it was all in the past, why was he so hesitant to make a commitment to the most amazing woman in the world? Maybe it wasn't all in the past like he'd thought.

With great reluctance, he followed the two men to the living room to hear whatever it was his grandfather had to say to them.

His brother sat on one couch. His grandfather sat on the other couch. Franco crossed his arms and propped himself up against the doorjamb. When Dario nodded for him to join them, Franco shook his head. There was only so far he was willing to go.

Nonno leaned back on the couch. He rubbed a hand over his clean-shaven chin. "I tried to do my best. I tried to raise your father to shoulder his responsibilities, but he resisted me every step of the way. He thought because we had money that he shouldn't have to work for things. I wanted to show him what it took to accumulate that money. Perhaps I pushed too hard." He hesitated as though his thoughts had drifted back in time. "No, that isn't right. I did push him too hard. I'd only meant to help him, but I went too far."

Franco stood perfectly still, afraid that if he moved his grandfather would be jarred out of the moment. And it was only then that he realized just how desperately he wanted to understand his father so he could better understand himself.

He had never heard his grandfather talk this way—never heard him admit to his own weaknesses. And yet he was acknowledging how he'd made mistakes raising their father.

"I didn't want your father to rely on others to take care of him. I wanted him to stand on his own two feet. I gave him every opportunity to find his way in the family business."

"Maybe he didn't have a mind for business," Dario offered. "I know that's not where my interest lies."

Nonno's gazed downward as he nodded in agreement. "I'd have to agree with you, but I couldn't see it at the time."

"But you just let him walk away." Franco's voice boomed with an anger he'd kept hidden for a lifetime—even from himself. He wasn't willing to let this subject go so easily. He needed to understand how he and his brother had been forgotten by the one person who was supposed to love them most of all. "You didn't try to stop him when he dumped his wife and two small children."

His grandfather's eyes reflected his deep regret. "I tried to reason with him. I ordered him not to go. When that didn't work, I begged him. And when he wouldn't listen to anything I had to say, I tried to bribe him. He…he took the money and left…left you, your mother, the business, his mother…and me." He lowered his face to his hands.

"But I don't understand," Dario said. "Every now and then, without warning, he shows up in our lives. He never stays long. He's like a distant uncle who just passes by and says hi."

Nonno lifted his head and met Dario's gaze. "That is something I never wanted you to know about."

"You've told us a lot already," Franco said, "so you might as well tell us the rest. It's not like we're kids anymore."

Nonno drew in an uneven breath and then blew it out. "Your father comes around when he needs money."

"And you give it to him?" Dario's voice thundered with anger.

Nonno's gaze once more lowered as he nodded. "I knew that way he'd keep coming back. I thought… I'd hoped he'd see what he was missing by not being in your life."

"So he never once came around just because he wanted to see us?" Dario wasn't going to let this go. Because they'd both hoped all these years that somewhere deep down their father loved them in his own way.

Nonno kept his head down as he shook his head. "I… I thought I could shield you from him—from his lack of caring."

His father didn't love him.

His father had never loved him. No wonder he'd walked away.

Franco was glad he had the wall to hold himself up. He'd had absolutely no idea that all this time he'd been blaming his grandfather for driving away his father, when in fact his grandfather had done everything he could think of to make his father stay.

Whatever his father's problems were, they appeared to be all his. Though his grandfather put on a tough exterior, he really did have a heart beneath it all. Maybe now they'd see a bit more of it.

But one thing was clear. Even if his grandfather hadn't loved them quite the way they'd wanted, he did truly love them. And that meant the world to Franco.

This revelation also told Franco that his assumption that his father had loved them and still let them down had been false. He hadn't loved them, and he didn't care about letting them down.

But the fact was that Franco cared a great deal about Carla—dare he say it, he loved her. It was the first time he'd had the courage to admit it to himself. And now that he had said it to himself, it wasn't so scary after all. In fact, admitting that he loved his wife was freeing. He felt as though he no longer had to deny all the joy and happiness that she brought into his life.

And he found himself admitting to loving their little baby. He couldn't imagine abandoning them. Even if Carla still wanted to dissolve their marriage, he wouldn't be far away. He'd be a part of her life as much as she'd allow him. And his son or daughter would become the center of his world.

Because his father had given him something else besides life. He'd shown him what not to do to those people you loved. Franco could do better. He would do better.

CHAPTER NINETEEN

AT LAST SHE could see her father.

A nurse showed Carla to the hospital room where they'd moved her father. The room was darkened except for a light above his bed. His eyes were closed as though he were sleeping. Her gaze moved to take in all the wires attached to him. Next to the bed was a monitor with his blood pressure and heart rate. She blinked away the unwanted tears. She would keep it all together for his sake.

Still, she couldn't ignore the significance of the situation. This was a scene she'd experienced more than once in the past several months. Each time it scared her.

Her fingers tightened around her purse strap. She just couldn't lose her father. She wasn't ready, especially now that she understood him so much better. This was a time for a new beginning for them.

She perched on the edge of a chair placed next

to the bed. When she glanced over at her father, his eyes were now open.

"There you are." He smiled at her. "I'm sorry for the scare."

"So you're all right?" She wanted to ask if he'd had another heart attack, but she just couldn't form the words.

"I'm fine. My heart is fine. They said I got a little too worked up."

"I'm sorry about that. I didn't think Franco's grandparents were going to show up or I would have warned you to stay away."

"It's my fault. I went to apologize to Giuseppe, but he thought I was there to argue about the past and things quickly escalated." His eyes reflected his remorse. "I apologize for ruining your big evening."

"It's okay. And you won't have to deal with the Marchellos any longer."

Her father pressed the button on his bed so he could sit up straighter. "What happened? Don't tell me that Franco walked out on you. Because if he did, I'll be having a word with him."

"No. I'm the one who sent him away." The memory of the pain reflected in Franco's eyes cut into her heart. She consoled herself with the knowledge that he would be happier if she set him free—free just the way he wanted.

"I don't understand. Why would you tell him

to leave? Did he hurt you?" Concern reflected in her father's eyes.

"No. He didn't do anything wrong." And then the truth about the marriage contract came spilling out. "And now...now I'm pregnant."

"Pregnant?" Her father's eyes widened. A moment later, as the information sank in, he smiled. "That's wonderful." When she didn't smile, he asked, "Are you happy about the baby?"

"I'm still in shock, but yes, I'm happy about it. However, I don't think Franco is. He never wanted any of this—a wife or a baby. After his traumatic childhood, I can't blame him. And now...now I can't tie him down with a family he doesn't want. I know Franco, and I know he'd stay out of obligation. That's not right for him, for me or for the baby. We all deserve more than that."

"Are you sure about all this?"

"Of course I am. Do you think I'd have told him things were over if I wasn't sure?"

"And Franco told you that he didn't want the baby?"

"Well, no. But he told me before about his broken family and how he never wanted to do that to his own children."

"That was just his fears talking, when he thought he'd never be a father. But he is now. Are you sure his feelings haven't changed?" Her father's gaze searched hers.

"Why would they have changed?" A spark of hope burned in her heart. Was her father just saying what he thought she wanted to hear? Or did he have a specific reason for his suspicion?

"I've seen the way Franco looks at you. He's a man in love."

"But the baby—"

"Have you asked him how he feels about the baby now that it is very real?"

"No."

"Then what are you doing here? Go find your husband and talk to him—really talk to him."

She went to stand but then turned back to him. "But I can't leave you."

"Of course you can. I've had a big day. I just need some rest, and tomorrow morning, if you want, you and your husband can give me a ride home."

Her eyes widened in surprise at his willingness to have Franco's company. Maybe there was hope for change. "Are you sure?"

He smiled and nodded. "Go fix things. I'll be fine."

She leaned over and kissed his cheek. "I love you."

"Love you, too. Now go."

She smiled. "Okay. I'm going. Be good while I'm gone."

And then she was out the door and headed for the elevator. She had to find Franco. She had to apologize for being so abrupt and pushing him out of her life. Was it possible her father was right? Was it possible this marriage had evolved into the real thing with genuine love going both ways?

He'd tried her phone. Numerous times.

Each time his call went to voice mail.

Franco wondered if she was ignoring him or if she was still at the hospital with her father. How was her father doing? Franco berated himself for letting her go alone. He should have been there with her, whether she wanted him nearby or not. But then he recalled the anger and pain reflected in her eyes right before she left with the ambulance. Maybe she did need some time away from him. That acknowledgment hurt him.

His first stop was the hospital. Even though it was getting late in the evening, he was hoping he'd be able to check on Carlo. At that hour, he didn't have a problem finding a close-by parking spot. He rushed to the front entrance of the hospital.

Franco yanked the door open and came to an abrupt halt. Carla was in front of him. Talk about good timing.

"Hi." He didn't smile. He didn't want her to think he wasn't taking everything that happened that day seriously.

"Hi." She didn't smile, either.

He backed up, letting her step outside. All his thoughts and practiced words became all jumbled up in his mind.

He drew in a deep breath, hoping it would calm his racing heart. "How's your father?"

"He's good. They said it was a panic attack."

"So no heart attack?"

"No. Thank goodness. They're going to monitor him tonight, and then he'll be released in the morning."

He shifted his weight from one foot to the other. "That's really good news. I'm happy for both of you. Do you need to go back now and see him?"

"No. He said he was tired and told me to leave."

Franco at last smiled. "It sounds like he's back to being his old self."

"Well, not quite."

The smile fell from his face. Just then another couple exited the hospital. They stepped off to the side to let them pass.

Once they were alone again, he asked, "What's the matter? What aren't you telling me?"

"Could we take a walk?"

It was a cool evening but it wasn't frigid out. And it wouldn't matter if it were snowing. He would have agreed to whatever activity that allowed him to spend more time with his wife.

They walked quietly beneath the streetlights.

He let her lead the way because he only wanted to be wherever she was.

When they reached a small park, she turned to him. "Can we sit down?"

"Sure." He didn't know if he should be worried or not, but he sensed she had something on her mind. Maybe he needed to speak up first.

"I'm sorry," they said in unison.

They looked at each other in surprise. Then they smiled.

"You go ahead," she said.

It seemed like the gentlemanly thing to let her go first. He'd waited this long—he could wait a little longer. "No, you say what you have on your mind."

"My father and I talked before the party." She went on to explain about his confession to cheating and how he'd meant to apologize to Franco's grandfather. She also told Franco about her father's driving need to see her married and that it had nothing to do with his doubts about her ability to run the restaurant business.

"That's great news." He was truly happy for her.

When she lifted her chin and gazed into his eyes, the moonlight twinkled in her eyes. It was as though a spell had been cast over him. His gaze lowered over her high cheekbones and pert nose to her glossy lips. They were so tempting—so ready to be kissed.

He gave himself a mental jerk. They were a long way from kissing. In fact at this point, he was pretty certain if he tried it, he'd get slapped down, and rightly so. He had things to say to her—important things.

"You aren't the only one to have a meaningful talk. I just left my grandparents' house. My grandfather explained a lot about my past— about my father. He answered questions I didn't even know I had." Franco leaned back and went on to explain that his grandfather hadn't chased away his father—that his father had walked out on his own family of his own accord.

"I'm sorry." She placed a hand on his arm and squeezed. "That must be so hard for you."

He shook his head. "It's more like a relief. I know that my grandfather truly loves my brother and me. He tried to keep our father in our lives. My father's actions were all on him and no one else. I really needed to understand my past, especially now that you're pregnant."

"I know I totally mishandled the situation with my pregnancy. I was so sure that you wouldn't want a family, and I didn't want to force you into a situation that would make you miserable—a family you don't want."

He turned to her. He stared deep into her eyes. "That's the realization I came to."

"That you don't want this? Us?"

CHAPTER TWENTY

HER HEART TUMBLED.

The backs of her eyes stung.

Carla blinked repeatedly. She sucked down her rising emotions. She'd promised herself that if this didn't work out the way she'd hoped, she wouldn't fall apart.

But when her gaze met his, her heart leaped into her throat. *Please don't say you want out. Please don't disappear from my life.* The words hovered at the back of her throat.

It wasn't fair of her to ask him to do something that went against what was in his heart. The worst thing she could do was force him to relive his past. She loved him too much to cause him any pain.

Franco shook his head. "No. That came out wrong."

"No, you don't want us? No, you do want us?"

His gaze met hers. "Before I met you, I was so certain what I wanted in life—I wanted to take over Marchello Spices and expand it."

"And now what do you want?"

His gaze searched hers. "You don't know?"

Her heart pounded so loud that it echoed in her ears. "No."

"I want you." His hand moved to her abdomen. "And I want this little guy or girl."

Tears of joy splashed onto her cheeks. "You do?"

"I do. I love you. I think I fell in love with you at our wedding, when we were dancing and you stepped on my toes—"

"I did not." She smiled. "You stepped on mine."

"Did not." He returned her smile.

"Did, too."

"Either way, I knew in that moment that my life would never be the same. But the question is, what do you want?"

She couldn't believe he was saying everything she wanted to hear. "I want you, too. I think I fell for you back at Gianna and Dario's wedding, but I was too stubborn to acknowledge it to myself or anyone."

"Ah, see…it was my dance moves." He smiled proudly. "They won you over."

She let out a little laugh. "Is that what you call what you do on the dance floor?"

"Hey, be nice." He continued to smile at her.

Her laughter bubbled over into a full belly laugh with happy tears in her eyes. It wasn't the thought of him dancing, but rather a release of her pent-up worries. Her father had been right— Franco loved her. Her heart swelled with joy.

Then Franco moved to kneel down on one knee. He took her hand in his.

"Franco, what are you doing?" Heat warmed in her chest and rushed to her cheeks.

"Something that I should have done months ago. I'm properly proposing to you."

"Oh." Her heart fluttered in her chest as her lips bowed in a smile.

"Carla Falco Marchello, I fell for you the first time we met in Lake Como. Your bright smile and sparkling eyes drew me in. But it was your caring heart and generous spirit that completely put me under your spell. I couldn't imagine living my life without you. You are my sunshine in the morning and my twinkling star at night. Please say that you'll marry me."

"But…but we are married."

"Will you marry me again?"

She knelt down in front of him and threw her arms around his neck. "Of course I will. I'll marry you over and over again. I love you."

"I love you, too." He leaned forward and claimed her lips with a kiss that promised love forever.

EPILOGUE

Five months later,
a small chapel in Lake Como

IT WAS A wedding do-over.

Carla never would have imagined that six months after saying *I do* to Franco, she'd be saying those words again and meaning them. This time it all felt right. Her father was there to walk her down the aisle, and she felt her mother's love shining down upon her.

Carla's hand moved to her expanding midsection. "I love you, little one. And so does your daddy—"

Knock. Knock.

"Unless you're Franco, you can come in." Carla turned back to the mirror.

She turned this way and that way in the same wedding gown. It had to be let out a little bit for her baby bump. There was something missing, but she couldn't put her finger on what it was.

Gianna poked her head inside the door. "It's just me. Is it all right if I come in?"

"Of course it is. You're my matron of honor." She glanced past her cousin. "Where's your husband?"

"He's changing Georgia's diaper."

"Wow. Impressive." She couldn't help but wonder if Franco would be that involved with their baby. If his current actions of attending all her doctors' appointment and helping to decorate the nursery in their new house were any indication, he was going to be an amazing father.

"I'm so happy for you." Gianna hugged her.

When they parted, Carla swiped at the tears of joy tracking down her freshly made-up face. "Everything is working out for the both of us. We've both found the men of our dreams. And we're sisters-in-law, cousins and best friends."

Gianna smiled brightly. "I don't think we could be closer if we were sisters."

"You are like a sister to me."

They hugged again. But Gianna quickly pulled back. "As much as I want to stand here celebrating all that is good in our lives, you have an anxious bridegroom waiting for you. We better get you down that aisle."

"I'm ready." She'd been ready for a while now. She'd been so anxious to say *I do* again and this time mean it with all her heart.

Gianna frowned at her.

"What did I forget? I keep feeling like I've forgotten something."

"First, we have to fix your makeup. Have a seat."

Carla did as told and Gianna set to work covering the trail of her happy tears, but Carla was quite certain there would be many more of those happy tears spilled today. A little cover-up and powder fixed things.

Gianna stepped back to admire her work. "You're frowning. Don't you like what I did?"

"It's not that. You did a great job. I just can't shake the feeling I'm forgetting something important."

"Oh, that reminds me. Your father gave me something to pass on to you." Gianna rushed over to the chair where she'd placed her beaded purse. When she turned around, she had a string of pearls in her hand. "Your father said you wanted something of your mother's to wear when you walked down the aisle. He said your mother wore this necklace on their wedding day."

Again the tears rushed to her eyes. Carla blinked and fanned her face, trying to keep her emotions under control so she didn't mess up her makeup again.

"Can you put them on me?" Carla turned around. After her cousin hooked the clasp, Carla fingered the pearls as her heart filled with love for those who'd passed through her life, those who were in it and, as her hand lowered to her slightly round abdomen, those who would soon enter her life. "Now I'm ready."

With her father at her side, they set off down the aisle. Whereas the first time Carla had married Franco, her knees had felt like gelatin, this time her legs felt sturdy and she had to restrain herself from rushing down the aisle.

This time when she met Franco's steady gaze, she smiled—a big, sunny, full-of-love smile. This time they were getting married for all the right reasons.

And their families were with them. His grandfather and her father were in the chapel without any arguments. Miracles really did happen.

And though their respective businesses were both important to them, they were no longer the center of their world. Their love and their growing family would be their focus. The rest of it would fall into place.

And when she finally stopped next to Franco, she turned to her father, who kissed her cheek. And then she turned back to Franco.

She couldn't help herself. She whispered, "I love you."

He whispered back, "I love you, too. Let's get married. Again."

* * * * *

*If you missed the previous story in the
Wedding Bells at Lake Como duet,
then check out*

Bound by a Ring and a Secret

*And if you enjoyed this story, check out
these other great reads from Jennifer Faye*

Fairytale Christmas with the Millionaire
The Italian's Unexpected Heir
The CEO, the Puppy and Me

All available now!